A FESTIVE FEATHERWOOD FALLS

FEATHERWOOD FALLS
BOOK 6

HEATHER REYBURN

Cover design: Patti Roberts (Paradox Book Cover Designs)

ISBN 978-0-6457440-5-7 Print Edition

Heather Reyburn

www.heatherreyburn.com

For my Mother - the beautiful soul who always ensured our Christmas was special

THE FEATHERWOOD COMMUNITY

In case you have lost track of who's who in this little town — here is a cheat sheet for you.

Ginny Shepherd begins this series as the owner and operator of "Featherwood Station". The cause of her husband's death (Lyndon) becomes clear after **Kirk Myer** arrives in the town.

Briony is Ginny's eldest daughter and we meet her Scottish partner **Alex Cunningham** when they get their own story in book 5 ***"Coming Home to Featherwood Falls"*** in the local hotel.

Claire is Ginny's second daughter who returns to the farm in book 2 ***"Secrets in Featherwood Falls"***. There she meets her partner *Rhys Morton*, the newly appointed police officer.

Lola and Frank Brown own the local general store and post office. Pillars of the community, they feature throughout the series.

Ryan Brown, Lola and Frank's son, arrives home in book 4 *"Clouds over Featherwood Falls"* where he reunites with his childhood sweetheart, Teacher's Aide *Emma Grey.*

Zoe Ferguson is Ryan's teenaged daughter – we also meet her in *"Clouds over Featherwood Falls".*

Nigel Ward is the owner of Glenrowan, the property next door to Featherwood Station. He features in both book 1 and book 6.

Ashleigh Paton and *Damian Cartwright* appear in book 3 *"Sparks Fly in Featherwood Falls"* when Ashleigh arrives in the town to teach at the little school. Damian's son *Charlie* and his great-aunt *Dolly* are also characters in this book.

We meet *Eleanor Worth* in book 4 *"Clouds over Featherwood Falls"* and get to know her better in book 5,

"Coming Home to Featherwood Falls" and again in book 6 *"A Festive Featherwood Falls."*

Sam Frankham (a New Zealand builder holidaying in Australia) *and Sophie Cunningham* (Alex's sister from Scotland) arrive in book 5, *"Coming Home to Featherwood Falls"*. In this story we also meet *Ciara King,* Sam's girlfriend when she and Sam are employed at the Featherwood Falls Hotel.

Bryn Hughes and *Francene West* arrive in Featherwood Falls in book 6 *"A Festive Featherwood Falls"* where we get to know them both.

1

Ginny stared at her feet, struggling to drag her thoughts from the overheard conversation in the local shop earlier in the day. She wriggled her toes in the pond and leaned forward to splash cool water on her face.

The kelpie at her side pressed against her as if in sympathy.

'Oh, Drum. Worrying isn't helping either of us, but what should I do if it's true?'

The dog's sorrowful gaze met hers, long, dark lashes blinking over his soft, yellow eyes. She hugged him.

She didn't feel old, but the calendar suggested she was not exactly in the flush of youth either. *Perhaps that's the problem—I misunderstood what was said and am letting my imagination run riot.*

With three weeks until Briony and Alex's wedding, and Christmas looming the week after that, she forced her thoughts to the upcoming celebrations. A prickling sensation surged behind her eyes, and she blinked rapidly. Ginny rarely cried—couldn't remember the last time she'd had a full-on sob. But lately things had changed, and she was helpless at keeping a lid on her emotions with this morning's revelations trying hard to push her over the edge.

Kirk's and her wedding had been relegated to the back of her mind while they planned Briony and Alex's big day. But then Briony had suggested that while Alex's family and all their friends were in Featherwood Falls, they should combine their services and celebrate both unions on the same day. It sounded feasible, but Ginny hated attention directed at her and being part of the huge fanfare for Briony as mother of the bride was as much as she wanted to deal with. Was honesty really the best policy? The last thing she wanted was to cause friction between herself and her eldest daughter.

A cloud scudded overhead, temporarily blocking the sunshine and dulling the sky to match Ginny's mood. Below, the valley baked in the summer heat, ripened wheat rippling as tractors circumnavigated paddocks and pumped grain through massive augers into waiting trucks. Lucerne fields glowed green with their hint of mauve flowers reminding Ginny the hay was ready to mow.

With leaden limbs, she dragged her feet from the water and rested them on the rocks while she reached for her wide-brimmed hat.

Minutes later, with the little dog at her side, she trudged toward the homestead, startling when her phone vibrated in her pocket. She reached for it and swiped the green icon, her heart lightening as Sophie's name lit up the screen.

'Hello, Soph. How're the tropics?' Ginny stopped abruptly, partly to interpret Sophie's broad Scottish accent and partly because she didn't want to lose connectivity—a regular occurrence on the farm.

'Och, Ginny, it's too hot for me up here. Sam too. He's loving it and has a good tan, but I'm being cooked to a crisp. And although we've enjoyed exploring this part of the world, we've decided it's time to head back to Featherwood Falls where at least the nights are cool, even if the days are not.' She paused for a breath. 'If that's okay with you, of course?'

'Absolutely. I'd love to have you back with us again. We've got a sheep sale coming up and could do with a hand.'

'Sounds interesting. Are you selling lambs?'

'No. The stud Dorsets.' Voicing her decision triggered a wave of sadness. She had managed the small stud for years now and adored her "girls"—the original ewes that began her foundation flock and were now too old to continue breeding. Clamping her lips together, she waited for the inevitable barrage of questions.

'All of them? Even Aphrodite and her friends?'

Ginny smiled at the horror in Sophie's voice. The young Scottish girl, soon to be Briony's sister-in-law, had fallen in love with the solid, friendly ewes as much as Ginny had years earlier.

'No. They will live out their retirement here. I already have a buyer for the rams, and the younger ewes and lambs will go to the sale in town the week before Christmas. With the early rain we've had, there's plenty of grass about and I hope to get a reasonable price.'

'I suppose that's farming. Sad when you form a bond with them though.'

'Yes,' Ginny said firmly, 'but I have to be practical too. The farm cabin bookings are increasing, Claire's riding business is flourishing, and as the hotel trade grows, Briony and Alex want to be able to call on me during the busy times.'

Sophie's voice softened. 'Of course, Ginny. But what about you? You're always doing so much for others. You must feel tired and cranky at times.'

Ginny's eyes widened in astonishment, and she slumped to the ground. How was it that a girl in her twenties from the other side of the world—one she had only met months earlier and hosted for a matter of weeks—could be so perceptive? Her own daughters hadn't realised how tired and out of sorts she had been feeling, or if they had, nothing had been said.

'I'm fine,' Ginny said, plastering a smile on her face and changing the subject. 'How's that lovely man of yours?'

They talked for a further few minutes before confirming that Sophie and Sam would arrive at Featherwood Falls the following Wednesday, then they said goodbye.

Ginny slipped the phone into her pocket and ran a hand over Drum's head.

'It'll be nice having Sophie and Sam back.' Her thoughts returned to Sophie's comments about her health, and she twisted her mouth ruefully. 'Perhaps I'll have a chat with the doctor when I'm next in town. And maybe it's time to stop being such a chicken and share my worries with Kirk.'

Speaking aloud did nothing to erase the words she had overheard in town, but she lengthened her stride, fighting the ache of dread.

'HEY, Mum. I've had another idea about the wedding and thought I'd run it by you.'

Briony's cheery voice at the other end of the phone was full of excitement. Ginny drew a silent breath and stretched her face into a smile before answering.

'Go on?'

'How about we combine our ceremonies as well as sharing the day—Kirk could walk me into the church and then return for you? Or we could both enter together ... you know, escort each other. Then we could stand as couples on an angle so the guests can see us both and take turns saying our vows, me with Alex and you with Kirk. It makes sense really, not only because of the guests but economically too. What do you think?'

Ginny's jaw dropped. She hadn't discussed Briony's ideas with Kirk and wasn't sure what to say. But she was certain most young women would want their wedding day to be all about them. Inviting their mother and her new man to join ceremonies seemed quite preposterous, no matter how close their family was. The Shepherd women had always been tight-knit, and losing Lyndon, Ginny's husband and father of Briony and Claire, had hit them hard. And while both girls loved Kirk, sharing a day as important as a wedding was ridiculous.

'Mum?'

'Sorry, love. I'm thinking.' She pressed her lips together, her disbelief mixed with a desire to burst into laughter. Fighting to regain her composure, she said, 'What does Alex want?'

'He's happy with whatever I suggest. You know

Alex. Nothing surprises him and I'm sure he'll see it makes good financial sense.'

'I don't think that would work but I'll talk to Kirk and get back to you?'

Briony groaned in agreement. 'Okay. But let me know as soon as possible so I can ring the church office and tweak the plans.'

'Alright. Talk later.'

'Thanks, Mum.'

They said goodbye, leaving Ginny leaning on the kitchen counter. Briony was the practical daughter—the business head and planner for the family in addition to being a qualified chef—but sharing her wedding day with her mother? Ginny exploded with mirth. If nothing else, Briony's suggestion had dragged her mood up a notch or two.

A black cat rubbed against her leg, and she bent down and picked it up.

'Teatime is it, Oscar?' After rubbing her cheek against the cat's soft fur, she replaced him on the floor and heaved a sigh. 'Okay. I'll feed you lot, do the outside chores, and cook dinner for us. By then hopefully Kirk will be home and we can talk.' She crossed the fingers of both hands as she opened the pantry door and reached for the kibble.

2

After dragging the trolley of rocks down the narrow tunnel and out into the sunlight, Kirk stood and rubbed his aching back.

Shading his eyes with his hand, his gaze roved across the valley below. To his left, the hill marking one boundary of Featherwood Station dipped away behind the band of trees, following the creek from the spring at the rocky outcrop on the horizon down to the rock pool amongst the ancient featherwoods. A sigh of contentment escaped him. He loved this place—every bit as much as Ginny did, despite only having lived here for a few years.

Pivoting, he stared into the cave from which he had emerged, a soft grin on his face. The silent, rugged, old mining area that held so many secrets provided an escape, and an opportunity to extract whatever minerals he could find to supplement his income—and for Kirk, that had been considerably more than he had expected. Because of the difficulty in reaching the mine and the fact that the only access was through Featherwood Station, he hoped it would remain that way, at least for the foreseeable future. Lifting his head, his eyes narrowed, focusing on the sheds surrounding the Glenrowan homestead. Slow-burning anger, often rising when he least expected it, crawled through his insides.

In the long run, he had been the only winner out of both tragedies. His tiny, premature daughter had been born sleeping and soon after, he had lost his beloved wife to cancer. But Ginny's suffering had been equally tough. Losing a partner in a farming accident was bad enough, but when the truth was revealed and her long-term neighbour had lost his freedom, the whole town had taken months to recover from the shock. Kirk's arrival in Featherwood Falls a year after Lyndon's death had been fortuitous. Ginny had needed help on the property, he had needed her permission to visit the historic mining area his grandfather had spoken of so many years ago, and over time, his and Ginny's friendship had morphed into a companionable, trust-filled love.

Despite both he and Ginny deciding marrying for the second time was not on their agenda, time had decided otherwise. They adored each other and the desire to cement their relationship legally had been a sudden but welcome surprise to them both.

Switching his focus away from the unexpected romantic moments that had developed over the past four years, he turned his back on the vista below, spread the rocks out in the sun, and inspected each one.

An hour later, surrounded by quartz-bearing rocks, he loaded the rejects into the trolley and trundled them back inside the cave before tipping them into the trench opposite his current worksite. Then, carefully chipping the chosen pieces of coloured stone, he selected the fragments of quartz most likely to bear gold. These he wrapped in pieces of fabric and dropped into a canvas bag. Then he stowed his gear in his backpack, ensuring his latest finds were safe in an internal pocket, shouldered the rucksack, and began the slow tramp back to his vehicle.

AFTER DINNER THAT EVENING, Kirk placed a bare arm around Ginny's shoulders and pulled her toward him as they nestled into the veranda sofa.

The thrum of diesel vehicles, their lights beaming over the land as they continued harvesting, joined the twitter of tiny birds settling into the shrubs for the night.

A cooling breeze encompassed them and Ginny leaned her head against him.

'Spit it out.' His voice was gentle, full of love and concern. 'You haven't been yourself for days. Is something bugging you?'

She slumped. Voicing her fears to anyone, even Kirk, seemed stupid now. *It might not even happen, so why am I so frightened?*

'It's the weddings,' she lied.

'You're looking forward to them ... aren't you?'

'Yes, but ...'

Kirk frowned, his bearded face wrinkled with confusion. 'Uh-oh.'

'Briony's got this crazy idea we not only share the same wedding day, but we join our two ceremonies into one. The services would be conducted in unison.'

His eyes widened as doubt crept in. 'Are you having second thoughts about marrying me?'

Ginny blew out a shocked breath. 'Of course not! It's just ... well, I don't like parties, or crowds much for that matter, especially when the attention is on me, and I'm too tired to bother with more fuss than Briony and Alex's wedding will bring without this latest idea.' She stopped and fiddled with the dainty ring on her finger—an exquisite band with two matching diamonds and tiny lacework engraved into the gold. It had belonged to Kirk's grandmother, remaining on her finger for over sixty years before she died, leaving it to her favourite grandson to one day gift to the love of his life. He had told her Katie hadn't liked it so he had bought her a ring of her choice and stowed the inherited one. Then when Kirk had asked Ginny to marry him, he had it strengthened and adjusted to fit her finger—and she loved it.

He grunted agreeably. 'I'm with you on that one. I'd rather nip into the courthouse and do the official stuff —and then tell the family afterwards. Let Briony and Alex have the whole day of celebration to themselves.'

She chuckled and squeezed his hand as anxiety faded. Everything sounded so simple when the words came from her strong, quiet and sensible man. *Should I tell him? No. Not yet anyway.*

'Perfect.'

'Come inside and I'll make us a cuppa. Everything is better discussed over a mug of tea, and I'm sure Briony will see it our way.' Kirk hauled her to her feet, wrapping his arm around her shoulders once more.

She pressed against his muscled chest, her face softening despite the uneasiness that turned her insides to jelly. Briony was the least of her worries.

3

———

Francene West stared at the tired, red-bricked building across the suburban Brisbane road, her hopes plummeting. She dropped her gaze to the piece of paper in her hand. The address was correct, but the photos she had studied online had displayed a freshly painted apartment with a cute patio facing east. The facade in front of her bore no resemblance to what she was now looking at.

She shrugged. *I might as well check it out now I'm here.*

As she glanced either way before stepping onto the road, a woman approached the building from the opposite direction. Wearing a cotton dress and a straw hat on her head, her thin frame bent forward as she trod firmly up the apartment block's concrete steps. Francene followed hesitantly, not wanting to give the woman a fright or distract her concentration. As she reached the last step, the older woman's foot caught on the edge and she fell forward, landing heavily on the tiled porch.

Francene sprang to her side and knelt, her eyes widening at the rivulet of blood trickling down the woman's leg.

'You're hurt. Let me help you.'

The lady looked up, her face pale with shock. 'Thank you.'

Francene hooked her arm under the woman's, easing her carefully to standing.

'I'm so sorry to be a nuisance. I'm getting careless in my old age and my mind was elsewhere,' she finished apologetically, patting Francene on the hand as she extracted hers and squared her shoulders.

'But there's blood running down your leg. You've taken a sizeable chunk of skin off and the wound needs cleaning and dressing.'

The woman groaned. 'Just what I need when I've got a big day tomorrow.' She pulled a neatly ironed and folded handkerchief from her purse and flicked it open.

'Do you live here? Can I help you inside?' Francene asked.

'Yes ... and thank you. Perhaps, if you don't mind, you could tie this handkerchief around the wound and accompany me to my apartment on the second floor.

The elevator is untrustworthy, so we'll have to take the stairs—and I don't want to leave a blood trail. All too horrifying for those who come behind, don't you think, not to mention the complaints our caretaker is likely to make,' she finished with a half-hearted grunt.

'Of course.' Francene squatted, studied the injury, and tied the cloth as neatly as she could without pressing too firmly on the raw wound, then wrapped an arm around the older woman's waist. 'Lean on me and we'll get you home. We can inspect it once you're sitting down.'

'Are you a nurse?'

Francene shook her head. 'No. I'm looking for somewhere to live and thought I'd check out this building before the open day on Sunday. There's an apartment on the third floor that's vacant.'

'Oh. That's directly above mine. It's the same plan and size, so while you're here, have a look and see if it's what you're wanting. Unfortunately, without a reliable elevator, the third-floor apartments are not popular, although now there's such a housing shortage, times are changing.'

Francene nodded and they began their slow progress across the ceramic tiles and up the staircase. *I've got nowhere to be, so helping her is the least I can do.*

Once outside the woman's door, Francene waited while she put her key in the lock, casting a quick glance around, uncertain. Should she be going inside?

What if this person was some sort of crazy lady whose loneliness made her do weird things like falling over deliberately to attract attention? She glanced at the kind face, shook her head dismissively, and followed the woman through the open doorway.

'Come in, dear. I'll sit here and we'll unwrap the handkerchief and see how bad it is.' She moved toward a pretty, floral-covered armchair in the tiny lounge room before turning around. 'I'm sorry, I forgot to introduce myself. I'm Eleanor. Eleanor Worth.' She held out a wrinkled, blue-veined hand.

Francene took it, surprised at its firmness. Now she was face to face with Eleanor, she estimated her to be older than she had first thought—possibly in her eighties?

'I'm Francene. Francene ... West.'

'I'm very pleased to meet you—and thank you for your kindness.' Eleanor gave Francene a smile and slumped into the chair.

Although small, the layout of the room was practical and there was lots of light. A kitchen filled one corner, with the sink facing the patio and low cupboards and a countertop separating it from the lounge area. A square dining table and two chairs occupied the opposite end of the space, its surface covered with an almost completed jigsaw puzzle.

'Do you have a first-aid kit?' Francene asked as Eleanor began removing the handkerchief.

'On the top shelf in the cupboard to the right of the stove.'

Francene followed Eleanor's directions, quickly locating the green package with a white cross on it. After placing it on the bench, she unzipped the cover and removed a wad of gauze squares, plastic vials of sterile water, tweezers, and a small tube of antiseptic cream.

With firm, practical instructions, and her leg resting on a footstool, Eleanor guided Francene's tentative ministrations, encouraging her to flush the wound and blot it dry.

'Don't be afraid, Francene. It's not painful and I have a big drive ahead of me tomorrow, so it's important we do this properly.'

Francene glanced up at Eleanor, her eyebrows raised. 'Will you be alright to drive?' *I'm not sure I would want to be your passenger.*

'Of course.' Eleanor studied the wound with a small frown. 'If you could tweak that folded piece of skin back where it should be first, I think a coating of the ointment and a light bandage around my leg will be perfect.'

Francene obeyed, surprised at herself. While not usually queasy in medical situations, memories of the night of horror nine months earlier flashed before her eyes. Her body swayed as dizziness threatened.

'Are you alright?' Eleanor asked.

'I'm fine. Sorry. Just lost my balance for a second.' Francene pinned the bandage in place and rose to her feet. 'Would you like me to make you a cup of tea or coffee?'

'That would be lovely, thank you. I don't have one of those fancy coffee machines, but if you're happy with instant, I think we could both do with a shot of caffeine. Don't you agree?'

Francene smiled, packed up the first-aid kit, and moved to the kitchen to make the coffee. Eleanor reminded her of a music teacher she'd had during her childhood—a well-spoken woman with a kind nature who'd filled Francene with confidence. She had needed it then, and she needed it now.

4

———

'The answer is no,' Ginny said gently. 'Kirk and I believe your wedding day should be for you and Alex. We would prefer something small, and the right time for us will come. Meanwhile, let's concentrate on doing what you and Alex want and we'll talk more about our choices another time.'

Momentary silence greeted her, surprising Ginny. She closed her eyes, willing Briony to accept their decision, fighting the distraction of the regular clunking sound emitted by the hay baler. With the heat having faded from the day and a dewy moisture creeping in, Kirk had disappeared into the paddock as soon as they had finished their dinner while Ginny made the call. *Please, Briony. I've got more to worry about.*

'Okay.' Briony's tone bore a hint of defeat, and Ginny released her breath with a whoosh. Once her daughter thought about her refusal, Ginny was certain she would recognise the differences in their lives and concentrate on preparation for her and Alex's wedding.

'Are Alex's parents staying here or at the pub with you?' Ginny asked, relieved to change the subject.

'They'll stay here, Mum. Bruce is dying to see how we operate and of course Aileen wants to spend time in the kitchen with Alex.' She chuckled. 'I'm sure she's keen to scrutinise her son's restaurant management, and I know that once the wedding's over they'll be fabulous back-ups for us while we catch a few days away—unless of course they accept Alex's kind offer of joining us.'

A spluttered laugh exploded from Ginny. 'What?'

'Yeah. It's true. He reckons we've lived together long enough not to worry about doing the honeymoon thing straight after the wedding. We can show them around a little of Australia and when we get a quiet spell sometime in the near future, we'll hand it over to Ann and Mark for a few days and get away.'

'Of course. Good idea.' Although not at all sure how Aileen and Bruce felt about the plan, Ginny was relieved that Ann and her husband had become such helpful employees as well as friends. Cataract surgery had brought Mark, the truck-driving partner of their stoic kitchen assistant Ann, to a temporary halt and in the space of two weeks, Mark had discovered the opportunity as relief bar-attendant at the Featherwood Falls Hotel suited him infinitely better than spending eighty percent of his life on the road driving. Ann's transformation from a methodical but droll kitchen hand to a cheery team member, who now laughed and interacted with her husband and their customers as though they were long-lost friends, had cemented the decision for Briony and Alex to employ them both full time following the departure of Sam, Sophie, and Ciara.

'I'd better go now, love. We've got to get the hay in before the moisture increases. Talk to you tomorrow?'

'Sure. Have fun.'

Ginny chuckled as she ended the call. It seemed only yesterday that Briony would have raced her to the paddock to prove her prowess at manoeuvring the hay loader, showing off to friends she'd brought home to the farm during holidays. Now her daughter was a busy and dedicated hotelier, about to marry the love of her life. Boring farm chores would be the last thing she would be thinking about. *Not unlike me at the moment!*

She thrust her arms into a light jacket, pulled on her boots, and strode down the track toward the lucerne paddock. In the fading light, the outline of the truck with the hay loader attached to its side was just visible. A warm flood of gratitude washed through her. Kirk had done the hard work—dragging the loader from the shed, towing it to the edge of the crop and attaching it to the truck—all before he tested the lucerne moisture and climbed into the tractor towing the baler. For a moment, memories of struggling to achieve everything on her own following Lyndon's death flashed through her mind. That had been before Kirk moved to Featherwood Falls—and before the truth surrounding Lyndon's accident had been revealed.

An icy shiver ran down her back. Increasing her pace, she hurried to the truck and hauled herself into the cabin.

'Forget that wretched conversation until you hear the facts,' she told herself firmly, turning the ignition key and releasing a relieved breath as the engine kicked in. 'Concentrate on the hay—it's far more important.'

But despite the brisk reminder, an uneasiness settled deep inside her and she knew nothing would dispel it.

5

Sitting at right angles to Eleanor, Francene perched on the two-seater sofa facing the balcony. Although the unit was far from modern, the furniture was classic, solid, and of a style that reminded her of the antique shops she loved to wander through. She sipped her coffee, reflecting on the strange circumstances she found herself in.

'If you don't mind me asking, where are you driving to tomorrow?'

'It's a long story but, to summarise, I have decided to move to the country—to a beautiful village on the western edge of the Great Dividing Range. I recently discovered it was where I was born, and during the process of searching for my heritage I have made some nice friends there.' She paused and her eyes met Francene's. 'I know it seems impractical for an old woman like me to move away from a city that provides all the health benefits we need as we age, however I have decided there's more to life than sitting around wondering if you're doing the right thing. The village and its residents make me happy—and the best part is that since the pandemic, many others have discovered Featherwood Falls too. So the town is growing, and that growth has brought new housing and the sort of community I enjoy.'

Francene blinked, a smile spreading across her face. She liked this woman. Her philosophy synced with her own. 'How lovely. Have you bought a house there?'

'Yes—well, it's in the process of being built. There was a small paddock right in the middle of the village. In the main street, actually. With prices improving, the owner of the land sold it to a developer who is now building four nice townhouses on it. Mine is one of the rear homes with an outlook over the creek and up to the hills behind the town. The front two face the road.'

'So tomorrow's trip is to check progress on your house?'

'Exactly. I shall stay at the local hotel. It has recently been purchased by a local girl and her fiancé and they've not only done a wonderful job of renovating, but they have become firm friends. The journey takes a little over three hours for me—including a stop for a rest and a cup of tea on the way.'

Francene sighed. Eleanor's new life sounded idyllic —the complete opposite to her own.

'What about you?'

Francene twitched at Eleanor's question. She didn't know this woman and wasn't at all sure she wanted to share even a smidgeon of her personal life with anyone, let alone a stranger. But something about Eleanor reassured Francene she was genuinely interested, so she swallowed her doubts and chose her words carefully.

'My husband died a few months ago and, for several reasons, I had to move out of our house. I'm not sure what I want to do or where I want to live now, so I thought I'd rent something small for a little while and see what happens.'

'I'm terribly sorry to hear that. You're so young.' Eleanor drew a breath as though waiting for Francene's reply, but Francene said nothing. 'Where are you living now?'

'Um ... staying with a friend.' She crossed her fingers and hoped she wouldn't be punished for twisting the truth.

'That's nice.'

Their conversation halted as each withdrew into their own thoughts. Francene glanced out the window as memories resurged and a stab of panic threatened to derail her. A magpie landed on the railing and began warbling, providing her with a welcome distraction.

Living in the country must be so peaceful. It was something she had never experienced but had dreamed about after enjoying that one special year—when she was fourteen and Marianne had been her best friend.

For a moment, she let her mind wander to the holidays when the two girls had stayed with Marianne's grandparents on their farm near Gympie. Feeding cattle, playing with the dogs, and riding one-behind-the-other around the farm on Goliath, the ancient Percheron horse, had filled their days. Goliath had been Marianne's grandfather's pride and joy in the days when he competed in the heavy harness events at the local agricultural show and was the one and only horse Francene had ever sat on.

They had both been devastated when Marianne's father was transferred to Melbourne for work and the family had followed. They had kept in touch for a year or two by letter, email, and texts, but as life moved on, their contact became less frequent and eventually faded altogether.

'You mentioned you want to see if the apartment above is suitable to apply for,' Eleanor said slowly. 'Would you like to look around this one now? After all, if it's not what you want, no point in wasting your time or battling with the hordes of lookers that seem to queue to view properties nowadays.'

Francene nodded, twirling a lock of dark-brown hair that lay over her shoulder. 'Thank you.'

Eleanor lowered her injured leg to the floor and carefully pushed herself upright. It took only minutes to show Francene the two bedrooms and bathroom-come-laundry that completed the apartment.

Adequate for her needs, Francene decided. Except its locality close to Brisbane city meant the rent was fifty percent more than she had budgeted for. Her heart sank, reluctant to commit to such a lot of what she considered "dead money".

'I can see you're undecided,' Eleanor said, her face kind with compassion. 'But I have an idea.'

Francene stared at her, her brow creasing.

'It's just a suggestion. You seem in limbo at the moment, undecided what steps you should take next—and I understand. My husband also died young, not long after we got married. If it hadn't been wartime and we weren't already living with my parents, I don't know what I would have done. Do you have parents in Brisbane?'

Francene shook her head. 'No. My mother is French, and after my sister and I made our own lives, she and Dad visited her homeland to catch up with family. Somehow that holiday turned into a year and now they've been away so long I doubt they'll return to Australia.'

'Oh dear. What about your sister—or is that where you are staying?'

'No. She and her husband live in Perth. We're not close—she's ten years older than me.'

'I see. Well, perhaps my suggestion might not be as silly as it sounds then.'

Francene narrowed her gaze, puzzled that a woman she had met only an hour earlier would offer advice or ideas to someone she barely knew.

'Why don't you come to Featherwood Falls with me tomorrow?'

The suggestion was so out of left field, Francene froze, unsure if she had heard correctly. 'I-I'm not sure.' Initial fear of leaving the environment she knew left her knees weak until a hint of hope wormed its way through her.

'Of course not, dear. You don't know me well enough—and I understand that taking your life in your hands in a small car with an eighty-five-year-old could be rather daunting.'

A giggle burst from Francene, surprising them both but easing the strained atmosphere as she considered the idea.

'Perhaps I could follow you? That way we each have our own vehicle and can be independent if ... well, if it doesn't work out.'

'Excellent idea. I shall leave here at eight in the morning, and I like to stop for a cup of tea at Aratula.

Would you like to come here to begin, or shall we meet somewhere en route?'

Blood pounded in Francene's ears. What could she say? 'Um ... meeting somewhere on the way might be easier. Means we can both concentrate on the traffic until we get out into the country.'

'Very well. Perhaps you would feel easier if we met at Aratula? I'm in no hurry, so we could exchange phone numbers and if you decide against it, you could call me in the morning. My phone is blue-toothed to my car so I can talk as I drive—very handy in emergencies, don't you think?'

Francene nodded, then reached into her bag for a piece of paper and pen. They exchanged phone numbers, squeezed each other's hands, and waved goodbye.

Glancing over her shoulder as she marched briskly up the road, Francene took a last look at the apartment building, her head spinning with excitement, eager to reach her small SUV and head out of town.

She seems a nice lady and I have nothing stopping me. And—no-one needs to know I'm unemployed and living in a tent.

6

———————

*B*ryn loaded the last of his possessions into the back of the Isuzu utility and closed the canopy door before locking both sides securely.

The pretty, dark-haired woman beside the vehicle thrust a container of chocolate-chip cookies into his hand and gave him a hug.

'These should keep you going for a while. I know you don't want to go to the farm yet, but keep Mum and Dad posted—please?'

He squeezed her and they shared a wry grin. 'Yeah. Just for you, I'll send them a text when I decide where I want to stay. And I promise I'll spend Christmas Day with them, even if our pain-in-the-arse brother drives me crazy.'

She chuckled and stepped back, holding him at

arm's length. 'You've come a long way and I'll miss you. But it's time for the next chapter now.'

He nodded. 'I can never thank you enough for the last two years. When I was lying in that hospital bed, I think I would have given up if it hadn't been for you—and your bossiness!'

'Do you honestly think I would have abandoned my favourite brother?' She gave him a small shove as he opened the driver's door and slid onto the seat, placing his walking stick on the passenger-side floor.

'And I feel the same. One day I'll be able to return the favour—and don't forget, I'm your number one "bridesman" when you and Ben eventually tie the knot!'

They both laughed, and she put her head through the window and planted a last kiss on his cheek. 'See ya later, agitator.'

'In a while ... no, I won't say it. We're adults now, right?' He thrust the vehicle into gear and waved as the ute rolled out of the drive. Turning onto the road, he yelled, 'Love ya, Mae. Talk tonight.'

As he drove away, he glanced at the slim, lycra-clad young woman in the rear-vision mirror, his heart filled with gratitude and love for his beautiful, bubbly, and caring sister. It had been almost two years since his accident and the long road to recovery had kept him in Brisbane for much longer than either of them had expected. The room in a house he'd shared with a workmate had been quickly filled by another resident when his prognosis was revealed, and his belongings packed up and delivered to his sister's home well before his rehabilitation had even begun.

He turned the radio up and tapped his fingers on the steering wheel as he cruised along the highway, the morning sun behind him and the misty-grey range of rugged peaks and hills ahead of him in the distance.

Despite the pressure from his parents to return home to the farm near Armidale, Bryn had politely declined, ignoring his mother's pleading. While still uncertain of the future and with no plan, he had opened a map encompassing both Brisbane and Armidale. Then he had calculated the distance between the two and drawn a tiny circle around the halfway mark. Outside the circle were the towns of Warwick and Stanthorpe, and right in the middle, on a back road between them, was a tiny blip called Featherwood Falls.

That'll do me fine for the moment. Time to test my capabilities and think about the future with no family influences.

It took only minutes for Francene to pack her meagre belongings and stow them neatly in her car. Her campsite was in the far corner of the grounds, not too close to the amenities but close enough for her to scurry across the grass before the early morning clank and screech of caravan legs being wound up, indicating the caravaners were on the move. Snagging a shower first meant not only did she get ample hot water, but she also had a mat to step out on that wasn't sopping wet or coated in talcum powder.

She turned to pull out the tent pegs as the sun rose, her mind tumbling over the previous day's extraordinary turn of events. A quiver of elation warmed her—she had never been good at making new friends and yet this woman had treated her as someone important, someone who deserved to be included in her own activities. A shudder ran down her spine as she recalled the first time Kyle had stolen her phone during the night and deleted not only her social media accounts but also her entire contact list. Her parents' numbers were the only ones she knew by heart, and she hadn't dared ask them for any mutual phone numbers in case Kyle overheard and had another hissy fit. It had even taken a disgruntled call from her sister, complaining Francene hadn't phoned her for weeks, for her to scribble the number down and hide it before Kyle found out. The most heart-breaking outcome had been the lost contacts of her friends. Some had been close colleagues since she'd worked in the bright and busy bakery almost a decade earlier, before completing her apprenticeship as a pastry chef—and before she had met Kyle and married him.

She shrugged as a triumphant grin flickered across her face. Thank goodness for miracles—even if the accident had been a shock. Now she was free and about to follow an eighty-five-year-old woman into totally unknown territory. *Am I mad?*

A wave of uncertainty swept through her, and she paused. *Should I be doing this?* Almost immediately, she dismissed the thought and tucked the tent into the corner of the car boot. With a last glance around her camping area, she confirmed nothing had been left behind, slid into the driver's seat, and drove slowly out of the campground. After stopping at a nearby drive-through coffee shop, she made her way onto the highway and headed west, turning the radio off and studying the scenery as if it was the first time she had ever seen it.

With more than an hour to spare, Francene pulled over to the side of the road in the tiny town of Aratula and parked under a shady tree. On the opposite side, a row of shops lined the footpath—a large fruit and vegetable store, a café, and an ice creamery.

As if on cue, her stomach rumbled. She grabbed her bag and stepped out, locking the car behind her. Trucks rumbled past, shedding a blast of hot air that ruffled Francene's hair and left a strong whiff of diesel as they went. After waiting for a break in the traffic, she hurried across the road, drawn by the fragrance of fresh bread and coffee.

A smiling woman of similar age to herself served her, delivering a perfect coffee with the frothed milk on top in the shape of a tree. With a cheese-and-ham-filled croissant in a small cardboard takeaway container in one hand and her coffee in the other, Francene forewent the tiny tables for a stroll around the village instead, hoping to immerse herself in the feel of a country town.

It didn't take long to explore the few lanes leading up the hill behind the highway, but with each step, Francene was stunned at the exhaustion consuming her. It was as though she was in a dream—one without stress, fear, and hopelessness—but one that allowed her to float weightlessly above reality. For years, she had lost interest in her surroundings and focused on simply getting from one day to the next.

She jumped as a truck horn blasted, bringing her back to the moment. With a glance at the empty take-away container and coffee cup, she dropped them into a conveniently placed garbage bin, hitched her bag more firmly on her shoulder, and strolled downhill to the highway.

A small silver car was parked behind hers, and a woman stood beside it, waving frantically.

Eleanor!

Francene had lost track of the time and glanced down at her watch, surprised to see it was only nine o'clock. It seemed she wasn't the only early bird.

'I'm coming!' she yelled across the street. 'Wait there!'

Conscious of Eleanor's eyes glued to her, she checked both directions to ensure the road was clear, then hurried over to be encompassed in a warm hug from her new friend.

THEY WERE SITTING at the rustic picnic table before Francene got a word in.

'How's your leg?'

'It's fine. I redressed it myself this morning after I showered, and I'm not bothered. It will heal quickly, I'm sure.'

Francene wasn't as confident as Eleanor. The older woman's skin was tissue-paper thin, her legs laced with blue veins. She shot her a small smile and hoped it didn't appear doubtful. *I'm no nurse, and what would a pastry chef who has spent the last ten years working in a boring office know?*

Eleanor unscrewed the lid from the flask. 'Is tea alright? I like to have a nice cup here with something tasty from the bakery, then have a comfort stop in Warwick.'

Francene nodded. 'Sure. I'm happy with tea.' She pulled an apologetic grimace and added, 'I was so hungry when I arrived, I've had a croissant already. But I'm happy to nip over the road and get us both something else?'

'Thank you, dear.' Eleanor fossicked in her purse and produced a twenty-dollar note, which she held out. 'Take this. I'll have a vanilla custard slice please—and you get yourself something too.'

Shaking her head, Francene gave Eleanor a dismissive flick of her hand and turned to study the traffic again before she crossed the road. 'You pour the tea and I'll be back in a jiffy,' she called over her shoulder.

As she tapped her card to pay, she straightened her

shoulders and thanked the shop assistant. Having complete control of her money still took her by surprise and she had to resist looking for Kyle's approval.

A wide smile spread across her face as she returned to Eleanor and their picnic. During the night she had wrestled with her inner self, reproving one minute for becoming involved with Eleanor, and the next, stemming the excitement that getting away from her past life might bring—even if only for a few days.

TWO HOURS LATER, Eleanor slowed as they passed a speed sign and descended a hill where a freshly painted sign read "Welcome to Featherwood Falls". Houses came into view, then a cute, historic general store with a post office next door.

Francene's heart lifted. Drinking in the scenery, she slowed to a crawl, keeping up with Eleanor while allowing her eyes to dart every which way. Bush-clad hills provided a backdrop to the village, with cow-filled paddocks and colourful crops rolling between the buildings and thick trees. Most homes were an older style, with verandas or wide porches facing the road, and more than one resident was pushing or riding a lawn mower inside their yard.

So busy was she absorbing her surroundings,

Francene braked suddenly, narrowly avoiding hitting Eleanor's brand-new Hyundai in the rear. She gasped, her heart racing.

Seemingly unaware of the almost-tail-end collision, Eleanor made a right-hand turn into the hotel car park. Francene pulled in beside her and jumped out of her car, staring up at the beautiful old building.

'Here we are,' Eleanor said. 'Featherwood Falls Hotel—our home for the next few days or as long as you want to stay.'

She beamed at Francene, rewarded by the widest grin Francene had shared in a long time.

A thrill of excitement brought pink heat to Francene's face. She opened the back of her car and slid her suitcase out before stepping to Eleanor's vehicle and unloading hers. 'Lead the way. I'll bring our bags.'

Without hesitation, Eleanor strode ahead, reminding Francene of a racehorse with the finish line in view. She rolled their suitcases along the concrete strip in front of the cars, startling when the front door of the hotel was flung open and a young woman with shoulder-length brown hair and a huge smile met them. She threw her arms around Eleanor then stood back, glanced at Francene, and extended a hand.

'You must be Francene. I'm delighted to meet you and thank you for coming to stay with us in Featherwood Falls,' she gushed. 'I'm Briony.'

Francene blinked, taking the proffered hand and shaking it with equal enthusiasm. 'Hi.'

'Come on in. Alex is preparing lunch, so you'll meet him soon. Meanwhile, I'll show you to your rooms, shall I?' She reached for both bags as Eleanor nodded, and with one in each hand, she almost sprinted up the staircase with Francene and Eleanor trailing behind.

The fragrance of lavender and furniture polish greeted them, mixed with the delicious scent of garlic and tomatoes floating through the open downstairs doors. Francene's mouth watered.

With a flourish, Briony opened both doors on her left and stepped back to allow Francene and Eleanor to pass by.

'This is the room I always have. You can be my neighbour.' Eleanor chuckled.

Francene gazed at the antique furniture, the brocade bedspread, and the quaint lace doilies on the dressing table. The room breathed pure enchantment.

Little by little, the pent-up stress she had shouldered for years began to trickle away, leaving her faint with relief.

I can't imagine a more beautiful place to sleep.

8

———

Bryn spent two hours in Warwick, enjoying lunch at a corner café where he could study the locals as they passed by. Although the café staff were helpful, he didn't stay. Instead finishing his meal quickly before taking a drive around the town and parking next to the Condamine River. Aided by his stick, he took a slow, measured walk along the footpath lining its banks. *A nice town, but not where I want to live.* Continuing southwards, he took every back road he could after first checking it wasn't a dead end, enjoying his solitude and stopping regularly to breathe in the scents and sounds of the country.

It was midafternoon when he cruised down the hill and pulled up outside a quaint general store with a fuel pump and a "Welcome to Featherwood Fall's Café" sign on the footpath. After parking, he reached for his stick and shuffled out, balancing against the vehicle while he rubbed the pain from his hip. The tablets he'd taken at lunchtime had barely taken effect, so he took another two and practiced the breathing exercises the physiotherapist had taught him. *I guess it's been a long time since I've driven this far.* After a few minutes, he hobbled toward the shop door and opened it wide, leaning on the handle as he stepped inside. A bell tinkled and a cheery-faced elderly woman appeared at the counter.

'Hello there. Welcome to Featherwood Falls.'

He blinked, paused, and tried to recall anyone in his life ever welcoming him into a store. Presuming the town was small enough for the locals to know every citizen who lived in it, a small smile hovered around his lips. A visitor to the town was clearly obvious—to this lady anyway.

'Hi.'

'Can I help you?'

'Umm. I'm not sure. I'd like to stay here for a night or two. Are you able to recommend somewhere?'

'Of course. There's the pub—a little farther along toward the bridge. And just out of town there's a nice farm stay if that's what you'd prefer? Featherwood Station has a couple of cabins and although I know they're booked for the school holidays, I believe at least one of them is empty at the moment.'

He rubbed his cropped beard, narrowing his eyes.

While a pub would offer hot meals and company if he wanted it, he wasn't sure that he did. A farm sounded more peaceful and somewhere he would be less likely to be stared at with questioning eyes.

'The farm sounds nice. Would you have the phone number please?'

'I can do better than that.' The woman beamed. 'I've literally just been talking to Ginny on the phone, so I'll redial while I know she's in the house.'

'Thank you. That's very kind of you.'

'Why don't you take a seat at the table over there? I'll bring the phone to you so you can discuss your requirements.' She moved toward a door on the back wall of the shop kitchen. 'Can I get you a cup of coffee while you wait?'

'That sounds lovely. Thanks. White, no sugar.'

'Won't be a tick.' She bustled to the coffee machine while Bryn ambled the few paces to the corner table and carefully lowered himself down.

A few minutes later, he sipped his latte while muffled voices sounded from beyond the kitchen and the woman returned and handed him a landline handset.

'It's Ginny. And yes, she has a vacancy,' she whispered.

'Thank you.' He pressed the phone against his ear. 'Hello?'

A pleasant-sounding woman responded and they

exchanged niceties before moving onto the details of his stay.

'I'm sorry. Not sure how long I'll be around. I guess it will depend on availability and how much I like the place.' He grinned as he spoke. He'd been in the town less than fifteen minutes but already felt as if he'd popped in to visit long-forgotten relatives. Still astonished by the store-owner's welcome, Ginny's had been equally welcoming.

He listened to the directions given, nodded, and finished the call. Before he had time to return the phone to the shop assistant, she appeared at his side.

'I feel terribly rude for not introducing myself. I'm Lola Brown. My husband and I operate the store and post office next door. Actually, our son now runs it most of the time with the help of a couple of locals, but during the weekends we do what we can so they can have family time together,' she babbled, her dangling earrings swinging wildly as she spoke.

'Nice to meet you.' He held out a hand and she took it in hers and gave it a firm squeeze. 'Bryn Hughes.'

'Lovely to meet you, Bryn. Now, I suggest you scoot up to Featherwood Station and get settled. Looks as though you could do with a rest.' She nodded toward his right leg resting on the toe of his shoe as he leaned on the stick. 'Accident?'

He nodded. 'Yeah. Couple of years ago. Taking a while for things to come good again.'

'Oh dear. You've had a rough time,' she said, her head tilted in sympathy.

'On the mend now. Anyway, I guess I'll see you again—and thank you.'

'You will,' she laughed. 'And you're welcome.'

As he shuffled into the ute, he could feel Lola's eyes on him. But for the first time since his accident, he didn't feel pitied or protected. Lola's interest was as genuine as her friendliness. A surge of unexpected happiness lifted his shoulders.

If the rest of my stay here is as positive as the beginning, this could be a really nice place to camp awhile.

TAKING a quick look at the town before he headed to the farm stay, he continued slowly past the police station, several wooden homes varying in size, to a brand-new complex of townhouses under construction, a school, and finally, the Featherwood Falls Hotel. Freshly painted and sporting tubs of colourful flowers along the footpath in front of it, the building oozed charm and history. Bryn's eyebrows rose a notch. *Someone's put in a lot of work—and recently, by the looks of it.*

Aware that Ginny might be waiting for his arrival at the farm, he crossed the bridge on the outskirts of the village and returned the way he had come, admiring the rows of jacaranda and silky oak trees lining both sides of the road.

A few minutes later, he paused beside the sign that read "Featherwood Station" and turned into a gravelled driveway bound by neatly mowed grass on either side. Ahead was a stunning stone and timber homestead. He parked in what appeared to be a designated area and before he had struggled out of his seat, a middle-aged woman wearing a smile and a long-sleeved blue cotton shirt greeted him.

'Hello there. You must be Bryn.' She held out her hand in greeting. 'I'm Ginny.'

He nodded and returned the handshake and smile. 'Nice to meet you.'

'I'm guessing you're keen to see the cottages.' She waved to a clump of shrubs against a farm track leading down the slope toward a woolshed. Beyond the row of brightly flowering grevilleas, he glimpsed a low building with a wide, wooden veranda. 'There are two cabins there. We call one Dandelion Cottage and the other Lavender Cottage. I thought you'd be more comfortable in Dandelion, the one nearest the woolshed. It's not as big as the other but has a lovely view of the lucerne paddocks and creek. I've opened it up for you and put clean towels in the bathroom.'

'Thank you.'

'As we discussed, you're welcome to join us for dinner or I can pop down with a tray for you around seven o'clock if that suits you better? Or perhaps you'd prefer dinner at the pub?'

'If it's alright, I'd like to have an early night. Haven't driven much for a while so dinner in the cabin sounds great.'

'Done. There's a basket of breakfast items in the kitchen and if there's anything else you need or I've forgotten, please ask.'

Bryn thanked her again, followed the directions to the guest parking spot, and unloaded his overnight bag and Mae's container of cookies.

Then he slumped into a wooden chair on the veranda, lifting his bad leg onto the wood box opposite, and stared down the valley in a daze.

What a find! The last two years had been hideous—a period of pain, inactivity, depression, and a sense of failure. But from the moment he drove into Featherwood Falls, Bryn had felt a shift inside him. A lightness and the hint of something he had thought he'd lost forever—happiness.

9

———

Since their phone conversation about a joint wedding, no one had mentioned the subject again. Perhaps Briony had also realised it wasn't quite what either of them wanted. Or perhaps there were simply too many other issues to deal with.

Ginny's weekend had been filled with haymaking —preparing Sophie and Sam's room as well as readying Lavender Cottage for the next group of visitors, baking up a storm to last everyone a few days, and participating in another of the ongoing working bees at the local church. Empty and forlorn for several years, the solid little building had worn a coating of dust and cobwebs, the surrounding grass neglected and rank. It had taken an enormous effort by the growing community to convince two denominations of church committees from the closest big towns to agree to return to Featherwood Falls and provide a service once a month. While many in the community would not attend, no matter which minister took their turn, there had been enough support and wedding and christening bookings for the committees to agree to giving it a one-year trial.

As a member of a foundation family in the area, Ginny had gathered a posse of friends and neighbours to clean, paint, and tidy the tiny church at no cost to any of the diocese. Briony and Alex's wedding was to be the first official event the building would host in almost a decade, and Ginny and Briony were both determined it would be one remembered and repeated by others.

While working on the farm, Ginny had caught sight of her new farm-stayer, Bryn, frequently visiting the stables and taking increasingly long walks around the tracks and trails as she had suggested. She had directed him to the falls, which seemed to have been his most popular destination, and although she didn't see him every morning, most days he reappeared around lunchtime from over the hill, his hair and beard damp from swimming and his skin a little more tanned that it had been the previous day. Opting to take care of most meals himself, he had only joined her and Kirk for dinner twice now—his quiet, well-mannered presence and obvious desire to keep his privacy providing intrigue. It was clear he had been involved in some type of accident but had volunteered no details, and neither Ginny nor Kirk had liked to ask. The two-night booking had been extended to a week and Ginny was disappointed she couldn't let him stay any longer as she had another reservation to honour. *Something will turn up if he's meant to hang around.*

WEDNESDAY ARRIVED and while Kirk raked a field of hay he'd cut days earlier, the sun crept over the range, spreading its golden glow over the valley. Sam and Sophie were due to arrive late that afternoon and Ginny flew through her morning chores, desperately trying to ignore her churning stomach. She had almost cancelled the doctor's appointment twice, convinced the only problem she had was the conversation she'd overheard and that certainly couldn't be helped by a doctor. Each time she'd picked up the phone to cancel, she'd halted, reminding herself sternly she needed to talk to a medical expert about other problems—the hot flushes, bouts of sleeplessness, and depression.

With only minutes to spare, Ginny dropped Kirk at the small animal market held every Wednesday morning and continued to the medical centre, where she parked unobtrusively under a shady tree a distance away.

An hour later, she returned to the car, suddenly aware of her surroundings and with a lightness inside her she hadn't felt for months. It had been difficult to begin with, but Dr Payne—an unfortunate name considering the woman was anything but—had put her at ease, chatting with more understanding and kindness than Ginny could have dreamed of. A list of recommended natural medications and options was folded neatly in her bag, but more than that, it had been the discovery of a new "confidant" that had helped. The only person she had ever discussed personal problems with was Lola, her closest friend, despite being twenty years older than Ginny. But Lola had been honest. She had been lucky and never experienced the midlife problems women talked of. "Talk to the doctor", she had said—almost three months earlier.

With relief and hope buoying her, Ginny headed straight for the pig and calf sale and sought Kirk out. Towering over the average man clustered around the pens, he wasn't difficult to find—and the two of them made their way to the courthouse. Instead of the usual crowd lined up outside, the old sandstone building was surprisingly quiet, almost deserted.

Ginny glanced around, puzzled. 'They mustn't have opened yet.'

As she spoke, a young woman emerged from the building before standing on the top step for a moment with a worried look on her face.

'They are open. Come on.' Kirk pushed the door and waved Ginny through before following.

Kirk leaned on the counter while Ginny fanned her face with her shopping list, grateful for the cool interior. Reflecting on her own mother's journey through menopause, a twinge of guilt flashed through her. She hadn't been particularly sympathetic, remembering the highs and lows of her mother's temper, but neither had she realised how uncomfortable this stage of life could be for many women.

'What do you think?' Kirk's voice disrupted her thoughts, and she blinked at the woman across the counter.

'Sorry. Would you mind repeating it?' Ginny stepped closer, training her concentration on the tired-looking face behind the counter.

'The dates on the licence issued to you last month are well within the requirements, so you can proceed with the official ceremony at any time.'

Uncertain of the woman's meaning, Ginny looked at Kirk and then at the woman again. 'So, are you saying we could marry today if we wanted to? Here?'

'Yes, and yes. There is usually a wait though. I'll check for you.' She clicked a few buttons on the computer and raised her eyebrows. 'We have vacancies on the next two Wednesdays or ... there is one at two o'clock today.'

Ginny stared at her. 'Today?'

'Yes. I guess that's too soon, but would you like to make a booking for another time?'

'No.' Kirk leaned toward her as he checked his watch. 'We'll take the appointment today please.'

A surge of relief flooded through Ginny, perfectly timed with another flash of hormonal heat. 'We'll do some shopping and be back.'

Then Kirk took her arm, and they strode out of the building in mutual disbelief.

Furiously fanning her face again, Ginny dissolved into laughter. 'I wonder who else does this?'

'Does what?'

'Does their grocery shopping before popping into the courthouse to be married.'

Kirk snorted and caught her hand in his. 'Probably not too many people we know but I'm happy. What about you?'

'Relieved and delighted in equal measure.'

By two-thirty, they were on their way home again, bags and boxes of groceries filling the back of the vehicle and the air-conditioning blowing hard against their faces. Now and then, they glanced at each other and laughed, each still struggling with the speed with which everything had happened.

With two witnesses they had never met before standing on either side of them, they had responded automatically throughout the official service and had emerged from the courthouse fifteen minutes later as man and wife.

Kirk turned the car stereo up and they sang to their favourite music as they travelled. Less than ten kilometres from Featherwood Station, Kirk reached out and covered her hand with his, giving it a warm, comforting squeeze. Taking their eyes off the road, they held each other's gaze for a few seconds.

Ginny was the first to look up, releasing a loud gasp. 'Stop!' she shrieked, pointing ahead to an oncoming police vehicle, its blue and red lights flashing as it came to a stop at side of the road. 'It's Rhys!'

Kirk braked hard and their vehicle slid to a halt. They both leapt out and hurried toward the police car, puzzled why he would stop on a bad corner where there was very little verge to pull on to. A gold-coloured utility was upturned in the table drain.

'Oh, God,' Kirk groaned.

She swung her gaze toward his pointed hand. 'The rego plate. It's Sam's.'

'No! No!' A sob burst from Ginny and she began

running, barely noticing the huge dead kangaroo on the roadside. 'It's Sam and Sophie!'

Kirk grabbed her hand as Rhys ran ahead to inspect the vehicle. As they approached the ute, all thoughts of their unexpected wedding disappeared in a flash.

10

———

'Help me!'

Sophie's moans reached Ginny's ears, and they raced to the smashed passenger side of the vehicle. Rhys shoved his arm through the window and wrestled with the inside handle. After wrenching it open with a relieved grunt, he flung the barely dented door wide and made room for Ginny to squeeze beside him.

Strung upside down by her seatbelt, blood streamed down Sophie's forehead and ran into her hair.

Gently grasping the girl's hand in hers, Ginny swallowed her shock. 'It's okay, Soph. We're here now and you're safe.' She glanced across at Sam, fighting panic. His solid, inverted body was crammed between the buckled roof and his seat, making it difficult to determine the state of his condition.

'Ambulance and emergency services are on their way,' Rhys said, easing Ginny to the side before reaching over Sophie to place his fingers against Sam's carotid artery.

He turned to meet Ginny's wide-eyed gaze and nodded. 'Pulse is good but he's unconscious.'

'Righto,' Kirk said as he leaned in as if to confirm Rhys's diagnosis.

The smell of diesel reached Ginny's nostrils. Turning away from Sophie for a second, she caught the worried exchange between Rhys and Kirk.

'We've gotta get them both out—as quickly as possible,' Rhys said quietly. 'Kirk, give me a hand with Sophie. Ginny, would you mind stepping back?'

Ginny obeyed.

'Where does it hurt, Sophie?' Rhys asked as he ran a careful hand over Sophie's arms and legs, pausing when she flinched as his fingers pressed into her flesh.

'My wrist—and my face, but I can wiggle my legs.' One eye was swelling, the cut on her eyebrow the source of the blood matting in her hair.

Kirk flicked open his pocketknife. 'Hold her, Rhys, and I'll cut the seatbelt.'

Carefully sliding his hands beneath her, Rhys released the pressure, allowing Kirk to slice the belt.

Seconds later, they carried her across the road and propped her against a eucalypt trunk. Ginny hauled a wad of tissues from her pocket and knelt beside her, mopping Sophie's face then pressing gently against her eyebrow as she reassured her that all would be okay.

Clamping her teeth together in an attempt to stop them from chattering, Ginny's head whirled. Consumed with shock, she prayed she was telling the truth. The smell of fuel was getting stronger.

From their position on the ground, Ginny couldn't see what was happening at the vehicle but heard the thud of something hitting the ground as the wail of a siren sounded in the distance.

Relief flooded her like a wave in a storm. She stood, willing the ambulance to arrive as Kirk bobbed up and threw an overnight bag from the rear of the upturned vehicle. There was no sign of Rhys, and Ginny presumed he was with Sam.

'Not long now, Soph. Looks like Kirk's rescuing your gear.'

'Sam?' Sophie's voice shook with anguish, her face so pale her freckles stood out as though they'd been drawn on with a felt pen.

Ginny sat beside her and wrapped her arms around her. 'Let's see what the paramedics say. Hopefully that's them approaching now.'

Sophie leaned her head against Ginny, silent tears coursing down her face, sending clean trails over the dusty, bruised skin and mixing with the remnants of blood.

As one siren faded, a second, louder one approached at exactly the same time as a car from the opposite direction.

'The ambulance and emergency services are here. They'll get Sam out now, so don't you worry,' Ginny said, her tone more reassuring than she felt. 'And Claire's arrived too!'

The Subaru halted metres from the women and Claire ran toward them, ducking between the fire and rescue staff.

'Are you alright, Sophie?' She squatted beside them, her face pale and her eyes wide. Leaning close to her mother, Claire whispered, 'Sophie and I were talking on the phone when the accident happened. I knew something was wrong when she screamed and the call dropped out.'

'I'm okay.'

'Lucky that young fencer on George's place noticed the ute head down the hill behind the trees. He told us he heard the screech of brakes then a crashing sound and realised something serious had happened. He rang Rhys straight away. I was arriving home as Rhys left.' She pointed to the emergency vehicles. 'He'd just called triple zero, and it looks like we're in luck as I didn't expect them to get here so soon.'

As she spoke, two farm utes arrived, and the scene

swarmed with farmers and uniform-clad first respon-
ders. Ginny hugged Sophie against her, grateful for
Claire's calm presence as she stroked her hand up and
down the girl's good arm while the injured wrist rested
in Sophie's lap.

A man in green overalls hurried toward the
women, squatting to face Sophie. 'Hello there. My
name's Lucas and I'm a paramedic. Let's have a look at
you.'

'Sam. What's happening with Sam?' Sophie
whispered.

'The guys are using the jaws-of-life to get the door
open now. He's had a nasty bump on the head, so we'll
be taking him to hospital just as soon as they get him
out.'

'Is he badly hurt?' Sophie's voice quavered with
fear.

'I can't say until we get him clear of the vehicle.
We've applied a neck collar in case of spinal injuries
and he's conscious again. The fire and rescue fellas are
working on it and once the guys have him well away
from the ute, we'll have a better assessment.'

While he spoke, he inspected Sophie's face and
wrist before reaching into his bag and placing a green
whistle between her lips. 'Suck on this for a minute
Sophie. It will help with the pain while I dress your
wounds. Then we'll get you into the ambulance and

once Sam's on the stretcher, we'll head to the hospital for a thorough check over.'

Rhys strode along the road with one of the rescue officers placing orange bollards every few metres, effectively blocking the road in both directions. Then he stood in the centre of the bitumen, his cap pulled down firmly, and appeared to scan the area repeatedly, his gaze swinging from the accident scene to the women under the tree and back to the emergency team, as though on autopilot.

A sound of twisting metal filled the air, jarring Ginny's nerves. Placing a shaking hand between her knees, she moved her arm from Sophie's shoulders to allow Lucas to bandage the girl's damaged wrist. She didn't want to leave Sophie but was desperate to see Sam. Was he really going to be alright? Lucas's detail had been professional but gave nothing away.

As though reading her mind, the paramedic glanced at both Ginny and Claire. 'Sophie will be fine with me if you'd like to reassure yourselves that Sam is being well cared for. The emergency team have made the area safe and are standing by in case of fire. Everything appears to be okay though, and there's no need for you to worry. Just keep back from the vehicle.'

Ginny glanced at Sophie, who nodded. 'Go. I want to know he's okay.'

'I'm here with Sophie, Mum.' Claire flicked a dismissive hand at her mother.

After a moment's hesitation, Ginny pushed herself to her feet and crossed the road to the hive of activity surrounding the gold-coloured Ford. A gurney stood near the driver's side and four men and a woman extracted Sam from the vehicle and placed him carefully onto it before securing him with numerous safety belts and moving him to safety. Ginny leaned over him, trying not to get in anyone's way but desperate for the reassurance that only Sam could give. His lashes fluttered open, and she met his deep chocolate-coloured eyes. A feeble grin greeted her, and she smiled back, a wave of relief weakening her.

'We're here, Sam. We'll follow the ambulance to the hospital.'

'I'll be okay. Sophie?' he whispered.

'She's across the road getting patched up but will be in the ambulance with you.'

He sighed and closed his eyes again.

With Sam secured inside the ambulance and Sophie sitting on a seat next to him, the vehicle pulled onto the road and headed to town with the siren wailing and lights flashing.

Claire laid a hand on Ginny's as Kirk approached. 'Don't worry about anything. Here's my key. Take my car and I'll take yours. I'll go straight to the pub and let Alex and Briony know what's happening then head to the farm to unpack the groceries and feed the animals.' Then she leaned forward and kissed her mother on the cheek. 'You need to be with Sophie and Sam, so go —now.'

Ginny needed no encouragement. Clasping Kirk's massive paw in hers, they sped to Claire's car and followed the ambulance in shocked silence.

11

———

Glancing at the dancing phone, Bryn placed the lump of wood and his whittling knife on the step beside him before reaching out and picking up the device. Then he drew a deep breath and swiped the screen.

'Hey, Mum.' After tapping the speaker icon, he replaced the phone on the veranda floor, stretching his stiff leg out in front of him.

'Hello, love. How are you? What are you doing? When are you coming home?'

Bryn chuckled and picked up the wood and knife again. 'In order, Mum. I'm okay, I'm sitting on my veranda whittling a little bird out of a lump of wood, and I've told you before, I'll be home for Christmas.'

For a moment, she didn't respond, and he glanced at his phone, thinking he had lost connectivity.

'I just wanted to hear your voice and know you are all right,' she said.

'I know,' he mumbled. 'I'm in a nice little town, and although I haven't been here long, this is a pretty cool place and both my body and mind are doing well.' Rolling his eyes, he focused on a tiny bird sitting on a branch in a nearby grevillea. It had been there every day since he'd arrived, filling the air with such a glorious song for such a small bird and posing perfectly for him. Bryn's fingers had itched to replicate it.

'That's good. Your father is looking forward to seeing you.'

There was a silent pause before he answered.

'I promised I'd be home for a couple of days over Christmas and I won't break my promise. I just wanted to find the right place for me to heal properly—at least until I'm more active and can work again. When I know what that looks like, you'll be the first to know.'

'You can always work here on the farm.'

'No!' He clenched his teeth, immediately regretting the intensity of his reply. His mother was a gentle woman who had done her best for her four active children. But no matter how hard he'd tried over the years, according to his father, his abilities and interest could never match those of his two brothers, Owen and Dylan. His father's voice had always worn a negative, disappointed tone when speaking with his third son, and over the years his mother had been helpless to change that. 'Sorry, Mum, I didn't mean it like that. You must understand that I can't live on the farm again. I can't work with Dad or Owen, and Dylan's only staying up north until they need him. I've got to find my niche in life, and you and I both know I've tried hard enough.'

He scraped fiercely at the piece of wood, fighting the cauldron of frustration and anger building inside him. The knife slipped, taking a chunk out of his thumb, and he dropped the utensil, swore silently, and pressed the bleeding digit against his thigh, watching the blood soak into his jeans with detached indifference.

'I know,' his mother said. 'All those jobs around the world and trying your hand at so many different occupations. I'm very proud of you for never giving up. But you'll be forty soon and I wish you men could just patch up whatever's bugging you. Dad and I aren't getting any younger.'

'Yeah.' Time to change the subject. 'What's happening in your life at the moment?'

While he half-listened to her ramble on about the latest Country Women's fundraising endeavours, Mae's upcoming wedding, the burden of cattle work, the problem with wild dogs having got into the sheep, and the vast hectares of hay to be made, he spun the handle of the offending knife in mindless circles on the veranda boards, letting his mind drift to the person who had gifted it to him and the reason he was now carving a wooden bird.

Having found a perfect branch of silky oak on the ground near the falls, he had carried it back to the cabin, dug out the canvas-wrapped tools from the bed of his ute, and begun creating. The bundle had been gifted to him by an old shearer years earlier when he'd stopped to help fix his broken-down vehicle on a dirt roadside in western Queensland. After Bryn had repaired the ute, the old man had held up twisted, arthritic fingers, his wrinkled face hanging like a basset hound's, as he regaled the story of the tools and the sadness he felt now his hands were too sore to use them. "Take them, son. You've got a way about you ... a gentleness that goes well with creating things. They'll appreciate living with someone like you." Bryn's heart had melted at the old man's reference to the tools being alive and he'd accepted them graciously.

They had sat in the table drain metres from the road for hours with a small fire in front of them and the billy hanging above the flames from a handmade steel frame. After the tea had stewed to a black liquid, the man sipped from his enamel mug and talked about the days when he'd been part of a thirty-man shearing team and spent his evenings using the tools to mend old furniture and create new. Eventually, he'd waved

Bryn goodbye and driven down the track. Their paths had never crossed again.

'Okay, Mum. I look forward to seeing you on Christmas Eve. By then I should have this leg working better.' He forced a smile onto his face before they said goodbye and ended the call.

Bryn inspected his thumb before pushing himself to his feet and limping into the kitchen. He rolled a piece of paper towel around his hand, put on clean jeans, and picked up his wallet, walking stick, and keys.

As he passed the grevillea, the bird trilled and flittered to another branch, bringing a smile to Bryn's haggard face.

'Thanks, mate. I'm going to the store for bandaids. See you soon.'

Grinning, he shuffled into the driver's seat and cruised down the hill to the village.

THE BELL JANGLED, and Bryn was startled by Lola's worried, pinched frown instead of the wide smile that had greeted him on his previous visit.

Raising his eyebrows, he hobbled toward her. 'Everything all right?'

She shook her head. 'Not really. There's been an accident. A young couple who used to live here.'

'Sorry to hear that. Anyone hurt?'

'Yes. Both of them, although it sounds as though Sophie's injuries are not as serious as Sam's.' Their eyes met as she sighed. 'Sophie is Alex's sister, our Scottish publican, and Sam worked with Briony and Alex for a few months too. They were on their way back to Featherwood Station—and nearly home.'

An empathetic stab of pain shot through Bryn. Although his injuries were not vehicle related, after his own experience he didn't wish any type of injury on anyone. 'Can I do anything to help?'

'No, thank you. They're on the way to the hospital now. Ginny and Kirk were returning from town when they got to the accident site. Now they're following the ambulance.'

'I wondered why I hadn't seen either of them today.'

'They called in here early this morning on their way to Warwick to pick up essentials. None of us expect something like this to happen. I guess Claire will feed the animals this evening.' She squinted at him. 'Has Ginny been giving you dinner?'

'Yes, but I'm quite capable of cooking. I've been lazy and enjoying her meals.'

'Perhaps you'd like a pie to take home for this evening? Save her the worry, that is, if the poor love has had time to think about it.'

He grinned and held out his injured hand. 'I reckon I need a box of plasters first.'

'Oh dear! How did you do that?'

'Woodwork—carving. Got careless and the knife slipped.'

'Come here,' Lola said firmly. 'I'll grab a bowl of water and we'll clean you up and get it dressed.' She paused. 'Speaking of home, are you staying on here? I don't mean to be nosey, but I know Ginny's got the cabin booked from this coming weekend and I wouldn't like to see you with nowhere to stay.'

'Thank you. Not sure yet, but I kinda like it here. I wouldn't mind finding somewhere local to rent for a while.' He rubbed his hip. 'Need a bit more time for this to settle.'

'I understand. Wait here while I get what I need. Janet will pop back any moment. She volunteers at the school for a couple of hours each week and today is her day.'

Bryn's gaze followed the energetic septuagenarian as she marched through the kitchen and into the connecting house, astonished at how much informa-tion had been shared in a matter of a few brief minutes. *I guess that's what they call the bush telegraph.*

The shop bell tinkled and he turned, expecting to see Janet—the middle-aged assistant who had served him on a previous occasion. Only it wasn't her. Instead, a pretty, young woman with glossy dark hair stood staring at him like a deer caught in the beam of head-lights. She wore a sleeveless summer dress that perfectly accentuated her vibrant blue eyes. Bryn stared back, mesmerised.

A tentative smile spread across his face then faded when she slipped around the opposite side of the grocery shelves out of sight. *Geez. I must be uglier than I thought.*

Lola reappeared carrying a small bowl, a packet of bandaids, and with a towel over her shoulder. 'Come with me to the side veranda. Probably not a good look to be doing first aid so close to the food.' Her frown had gone and she smiled, her earrings jingling. As they moved toward the door, the girl emerged from behind the magazine stand, catching both Bryn's and Lola's attention.

'Hello, Francene. I'm sorry, I didn't realise you were there.' She rested a hand on Bryn's arm for a second. 'Would you mind if I serve Francene before we look at that wound?'

He shook his head. How could he possibly consider his needs before someone as gorgeous as Francene.

'I-I was wondering if you sold books?' Her voice was soft with a hint of nervousness.

'I'm sorry, love. Lots of magazines to choose from, but no books. The mobile library comes through each week, you see—and people drive in and out to town now as though it's only a couple of k's away.'

'Oh.' She glanced down at the magazine she held

in her hand—a thick, quarterly copy of a rural publication featuring women. 'I'll take this then. It looks interesting.'

'Good on you, love.'

'Is there a book exchange in the village?' Francene asked.

'Unfortunately, no. I've thought about that a few times. They're not a bad idea, are they?' Lola nodded thoughtfully as she punched in the purchase details and waited for Francene to tap her card. 'I'm sure most of us have shelves of books we've read and won't read again. That might be something Frank could set up. He's a pretty good handyman and we've got plenty of timber in the shed.'

'Okay, thanks.' Francene turned away as if to leave.

'Francene. I apologise—I didn't introduce you to Bryn here. Arrived in Featherwood Falls last Friday. Same day as you, wasn't it?' She swung her gaze from one to the other. 'You've probably already met.'

Their eyes held for a few seconds before Francene said, 'No, we haven't. Hi.'

'Gidday,' he replied, kicking himself for being such an awkward dork.

Francene looked back at Lola. 'Thanks again. See you next time.' And then she was gone.

They watched her cross the road and head toward the hotel.

'Such a sweet young woman,' Lola said. 'It's nice

having new people in town, but ...' She heaved a sigh. 'Like you, she's probably just passing through—more's the pity.' She flapped a hand toward the side veranda. 'Come on. Let's get this thumb of yours sorted out. I've got Briony coming in a few minutes for a fitting.'

Bryn followed the older woman, her words "More's the pity" hanging in his mind and with no idea what she meant by Briony's fitting. Would she be happy with both him and Francene living in the village—and if so, was that a sentiment felt by the entire community? So far, he hadn't been farther than Featherwood Station and the general store. Apart from Lola, Frank, Janet and Ryan, Bryn had only met Ginny, Kirk, and Claire. He found it hard to believe everyone in the village was as friendly as they were. Francene hadn't exactly oozed approachability, confirming his suspicions.

He straightened and shot a glance over his shoulder, catching sight of a blue dress fluttering as Francene disappeared from sight.

Maybe Featherwood Falls has got more to offer than I expected—including challenges.

12

———

Striding along the footpath, Francene's thoughts rested on the man she had just met. Despite his smile, there was a hint of sadness in his eyes—a trace of despair almost. Perhaps his injured hand was giving him a lot of pain. Or maybe it had something to do with the walking stick he leaned so heavily on. Or perhaps, like her, there were broken pieces within him that needed fixing and he didn't know how. She dismissed her thoughts, pushing the vision of the man out of her mind. One dysfunctional relationship in her life had been enough. The last thing she was interested in was another.

The sun beat down on her bare head and she wished she'd thought to wear her hat. Since arriving in the small town, Eleanor had taken her under her wing —insisting they inspect the progress of her under-construction house each morning before taking one of the delicious, packed picnic baskets from the hotel and driving around the district, stopping to inspect every waterway, historic building, gift shop, and anything else the older woman considered worthy of a visit. Today though, Eleanor had gone to Tenterfield to visit an old friend—someone who had helped her find her ancestry, and with it, her birthplace … Featherwood Falls.

Despite the gratitude Francene felt toward Eleanor, who hadn't displayed a speck of "crazy-ladyness", Francene fancied wandering around the village and spending the afternoon under a tree beside the local waterhole, reading. She glanced again at the magazine in her hand.

Oh well, you'll have to do.

Instead of scurrying along the path with her head down as she had done for years, she lifted her chin and drew a deep breath. The air felt clean and smelled of flowers and freshly cut grass. No hint of traffic fumes and only the occasional vehicle that cruised through or stopped in the town.

Halfway between the shop and hotel, a small car was parked in front of a pretty timber cottage. A woman stepped out of it dressed in a red skirt and white blouse, looking smart and efficient, her clothing perfectly matching the colour of the car. Francene slowed her stride, observing the woman wrestling something from the boot of the vehicle. A large sign. Carrying it in one hand with a small fabric bag in the other, she leaned the placard against the fence and wiped her forehead, staring straight at Francene.

'Hello,' she said brightly.

'Hi.' Francene couldn't help returning the friendly grin and paused, inspecting the "For Sale" sign in bright red letters. She glanced at the cottage, studying it closely.

'Interested?' the woman asked.

Francene shrugged. 'Not really. Just visiting.'

'I don't think this one will take long to sell. Deceased estate, and until recently it was well cared for and maintained.'

Francene breathed in the freshly mown lawn clashing with the weed-filled garden along the front of the house. 'And now?'

'Still nice inside and I've had a chap mow the grass, but it needs a bit of love.' She stared at Francene and held out her hand. 'I'm Pam Triller, real estate agent.'

Francene ran her palm down the side of her dress and grasped Pam's. 'Francene West.' She pointed to the sign. 'Would you like me to hold that for you while you fix it to the fence? Presuming that's what you're planning to do, of course.'

'Thank you.' Pam beamed. 'It's so much easier with two.'

With a screwdriver and four screws from within the

fabric bag, it took only a few minutes to attach the board to the white-painted pickets.

'I've got to do a quick inside check and make sure nothing unexpected has taken up residence. Would you like to have a peep?'

Francene's eyes widened at the invitation, hesitating in confusion. Did Pam think she looked like a prospective buyer? Or was she simply being friendly? A group of children rode by on their bikes, waving and calling out a hello as they passed. Francene's guard softened. *No harm in having a look I suppose.*

She followed Pam up the steps onto the wide front veranda wrapping around two sides of the building as though giving the weatherboard walls a hug. Above them, a corrugated roof extended from the base of the steep gable to beyond the veranda posts, shading the entire building from both sun and weather, while underfoot, wide timber boards formed the floor, their scuffed, grey patina desperate for a coat of oil.

A sliver of nostalgia ran through her, memories of the old homestead where she and Marianne had stayed as teenagers. It had been similar—only bigger and surrounded by paddocks instead of other homes.

Pam marched in and out of each room, checking windows and doors operated as they should and that nothing had been left in the cupboards. Francene drifted behind her, letting the ambience of the old home soak into her soul and imagining days when children's laughter and cheerful chatter filled the rooms.

Although only a small building, it contained two bedrooms and a large, square front room with a relatively new combustion fire. *The lounge?* Most furniture had been removed, leaving only a silky-oak wardrobe in each bedroom and a solid square table and four chairs in the centre of the kitchen. At some time in the building's history, a wall between what might have been the dining or third bedroom had been removed, leaving the kitchen as a roomy L-shape with a back door opening onto another veranda.

In Pam's wake, Francene stepped out, peering over Pam's shoulder at the surprisingly new bathroom at one end of the porch and a toilet and small laundry at the other.

'Nice layout, really,' Pam said. 'For a couple anyway. Might be a bit small for a family.'

'I love the kitchen,' Francene said. 'The wood stove looks well used and would be nice in winter. I've been told it gets pretty cold here?'

'Oh yes. This is frosty country for three or four months of the year and I've no doubt this would have been where the couple spent most of their days.'

'How long ago did they move out?'

'Mrs Walker passed away about a year ago and her husband tried to keep going. But his health wasn't good and a few weeks ago he fell and broke a hip. The family put him in care once he came out of hospital, but I think he'd lost the will to live. Joined his wife again, and now the family has said they have no intention of coming to live here and want the place sold. So … to answer your question, the house has only been vacant for about a month.'

'So, the Walkers were happy here then?'

'Evidently so. I believe they ran a newsagency in Brisbane somewhere but retired here for a quiet country life. Anyway, it looks like everything is clean and there's no sign of pests—so I'll get on and arrange an *open home.*'

As Francene reached the cottage gate, she studied the sign before turning back to Pam who was locking the door.

'Pam, what's the asking price?'

A lungful of air whooshed from her at Pam's response. Less than half of anything she had found in Brisbane, even in one of the less popular suburbs.

'Thank you.' Hope flooded through her like a rising tide. *Is this my chance to change my life?* Then practicality returned and her heart plummeted. *Don't be ridiculous. What would you do to earn a living way out here?*

While juggling mixed emotions, she shot Pam a smile. 'I'd better get on now. Thanks for letting me have a look at the house.'

'You're welcome. You might know someone who's

interested.' She handed Francene a card. 'Here's my contact details in case you want to pass them on.'

They said goodbye and Francene continued toward the hotel, her head in a whirl of dreams, hopes, and ideas.

Metres from the hotel, Briony greeted her, her face pink and flustered.

'Hi, Francene. Sorry, can't stop to chat. I'm running late for my fitting.'

'No worries. Hope everything's perfect for you.'

They exchanged a smile and continued on their respective journeys, Briony's comment belonging to another world from Francene's. Francene pondered her own situation. *What am I thinking? I've been living in a tent and currently don't have a job. Should I be honest and talk to someone about it?*

She shook her head. She wasn't ready to share her secrets. Not yet anyway.

ON ARRIVAL AT THE HOTEL, Francene was about to head to her room for her sunhat when a crash sounded from the kitchen. She paused, listening for a call for help. There was a Scottish-accented expletive, but nothing more. She grinned and followed the voice, crossing the empty dining room and standing in the kitchen doorway, unwilling to enter uninvited.

'Is everything alright?'

'Och, Francene. I'm sorry if you overheard me.' Alex met her gaze red-faced. 'Briony's gone to try on her wedding dress, it's Ann's day off and we had some alarming news this afternoon about my sister. She's okay. But I thought I'd whip up some chocolate eclairs for dessert tonight and would you believe it, the wretched piping bag just burst. I tried to stop the dough from going everywhere and knocked the tray onto the floor in my haste.'

Francene's mouth twitched with sympathetic amusement. Choux pastry mix sat in a buttery blob on the workbench, the offending piping bag disgorging the last of its contents onto the stainless steel while a tray lay upturned at Alex's feet.

'Let me help.' She dropped the magazine on a side bench, strode to the sink in the kitchen's corner, scrubbed her hands, and reached for a clean bowl from the shelf above Alex. Then, in the space of a few seconds, she scooped the dough into the bowl.

'The bench is clean so this will be reusable. Have you got more piping bags?'

Their eyes met, his wide in astonishment. 'Thanks, Francene. Um. Yes, there's a packet of them in the pantry.'

'Do you mind if I help?' A hot wave of embarrass-ment suddenly encompassed her. 'I mean, I'm happy to leave you to it if you'd prefer.'

Alex shook his head wordlessly, pointing to the packet in the pantry. 'You've done this before?'

Francene angled her head. 'A few times,' she said shyly. 'I like to cook.'

While she retrieved the nozzle from the split bag, then washed, dried, and inserted it into the new one, Alex cleaned up the mess on the floor and rinsed the oven tray.

Soon after, a full tray of neatly piped éclair dough waited beside the stove for baking.

Clearly still surprised by her assistance, Alex had barely said a word. As she'd worked, she felt his eyes boring into her, focusing on her deft movements.

'Will that be enough?' Francene asked.

'Thanks heaps. Yes, you saved my blood pressure—and curbed my coarse language.'

She laughed for the first time in months. It felt strange, even to her own ears. 'You're welcome. Any time you need a hand while I'm staying here, just ask. I'd love to help.' Then she shot him another smile, picked up her magazine, and walked out of the kitchen.

She took the stairs two at a time, her heart singing and her mind racing.

I can still do it! Like riding a bike or learning to swim, I haven't lost it. Oh my goodness! I want to stay.

13

It was eleven o'clock that evening before Ginny and Kirk returned to Featherwood Station and walked up the path with a tired, pale Sophie between them.

Claire, Briony, and Alex greeted each of them with a hug, the Scotsman holding Sophie carefully before stepping back and surveying her injuries.

'Are you okay?' Briony asked.

'Yeah. A few bruises.' Sophie gave a small smile and lifted her plastered left arm. 'And a broken wrist and stitches in my eyebrow, but otherwise I'm grand.'

'And Sam?'

'He's going to be okay. They're keeping him in for a day or two because of concussion, but he has nothing broken so they reckon he'll be fine.' Ginny met her daughter's questioning expression.

'Are they sure?' Claire said. 'I saw the ute when the truck came to get it. It's pretty smashed up.'

'It's a miracle—but now we have Sophie home and Sam's being well cared for, we could all do with a good cup of tea then sleep.'

'I made mushroom risotto. Wasn't sure how hungry you'd be?' Claire said. 'Rhys has already been. He spent a while at the scene investigating and cleaning up then came here for dinner and is now back at the station catching up with reports—but he left plenty for you guys.'

Kirk grinned, leading the procession up the steps and into the living area. 'I don't know about the girls, but I'm starving. Risotto sounds perfect.'

'Thanks, love.' Ginny rolled her eyes. 'Kirk nipped out and bought us a pizza ... but evidently that didn't fill the gap.'

'We were worried about you both, Sophie,' Alex said quietly, his hand resting on Sophie's.

She smiled softly and placed a kiss on his cheek. 'Thanks, Al. I'll be fine and so will Sam. You look as tired as I feel, so why don't you and Briony go home now? We'll catch up tomorrow.'

Briony and Alex hugged her again before saying goodbye to the family and heading out into the dark.

Sophie, Kirk, and Ginny enjoyed their risotto before Claire left for home, then the three of them curled up on the veranda in the cooling night air.

Despite her exhaustion, Sophie seemed to want to talk —to revisit the entire terrifying afternoon—so Ginny and Kirk let her share her story.

'We didn't see the kangaroo until it was too late.' Her voice quivered. 'And when I felt the bang and the ute started to roll, I thought we were both about to die.' A sob escaped from her, and Ginny held her slight frame against her own curvy warmth.

'I can imagine how terrified you would have been. But everything's alright now. You're both safe and will heal,' she soothed.

'What about Mum and Dad!' Sophie wailed. 'Do they know? Has Alex rung them? And I'm supposed to be a bridesmaid in just over two weeks—how can I do it with a cast on my arm and bruises all over my face?'

'It's okay, Soph. We'll ring your mum and dad tomorrow once we've all had a good sleep and we know how Sam's doing. They'll be busy trying to pack and get everything organised at home, knowing it will be weeks before they return. By the time they arrive here, your bruises will have faded and your stitches will be out. Let's not worry them unnecessarily. As for the wedding—makeup will cover most things and your bouquet will do a good job of hiding the cast in the photos.'

Sophie sighed, calmer now. 'You're right. Perhaps not such a good idea to video call yet.'

Both Ginny and Kirk nodded in agreement.

Sophie bowed her head and plucked at the hem of her shorts then lifted her chin sharply, staring at Ginny first and then Kirk. 'Ginny! You're wearing a wedding ring?'

'I am. Kirk and I were married today.'

Despite the emotional and traumatic day, a warm tingle ran through her as she looked down at her hand. A hasty visit to the jeweller's between making the courthouse reservation and buying groceries had secured a plain gold ring that fitted and that had been all they needed.

Her injuries suddenly forgotten, Sophie leapt up and hugged them both with her good arm. 'That's wonderful! Congratulations.'

Ginny's insides squeezed. Normally her own daughters would have been the first to know ... but, with all that had happened, nothing about the day seemed normal now, not even their wedding. As quickly as her concerns rose, they faded again as Sophie's obvious joy joined her own.

With Sophie in a better state of mind, Ginny helped her unpack what she needed and get into bed.

Later, Ginny stood under a hot shower, the events of the day playing over and over in her head. Concern for Sam and Sophie alternated with elation and shock about her own wedding ceremony. With a smile on her face, she turned the water off and stepped out before towelling herself briskly. Then, as she reached for her toothbrush, the one thing that had bothered her for days resurfaced. *That blasted conversation.* She had to talk to her nephew, Andrew. Surely, he would know what was happening.

IT WAS after eight the following morning before Ginny woke and dragged herself to the kitchen. Kirk's empty coffee cup sat in the sink, confirmation that he was up and, hopefully, had fed the animals and would be in for breakfast any minute.

She cracked eggs into a bowl and set the pan on the stove as uneven footsteps sounded on the paved pathway.

Leaving her preparation, she hurried to the front veranda. 'Bryn. How are you? I'm sorry I didn't get a chance to talk yesterday.'

'That's okay, Ginny. Lola said you'd gone to town and told me about the accident, so I knew it could be a late one for you.'

'Come in. I'm about to cook breakfast. Would you like to join us?'

'Thanks, but I've already eaten.' He hesitated. 'Have you got a minute to talk?'

'Of course, just a second while I turn the stove off.'

He lay his stick on the veranda floor and hobbled

to the chair Ginny indicated as she reached to switch off the hotplate.

She returned to sit opposite him. 'Is something bothering you?'

He drew a deep breath and Ginny groaned inwardly. The upcoming conversation didn't appear to be a light one.

'I know I can only stay until the end of the week. But ... I really like it here and would like to hang around a bit longer. I was wondering if you knew of anyone who might have a place I can rent?'

Ginny's eyebrows lifted. It wasn't the first time guests had wanted to extend their holiday. Several had stayed regularly while their house was being built or renovated, but this was the first time she'd had a single man stay since Kirk—one who wanted to live in the area.

'I'm not sure what's available in town. Lola would probably know. Did you ask her yesterday?'

This time he shook his head, his lips pressed together for a long moment.

'What sort of place are you looking for?'

'I'm not sure I want to be in town. I enjoy doing woodwork, you see, and thought perhaps someone might have a farm cottage or something similar with a shed I could use?'

Lost for words, Ginny wracked her brains for some way she could help this nice man. Then she remembered Claire's parting comment the previous evening. Months earlier, Claire and Rhys had bought Kirk's property from him when he moved into the homestead with Ginny in the hope the promised second police officer would arrive in Featherwood Falls within the next year. That would allow them to move out of the cramped police quarters and live in their own home. Meanwhile, they had refreshed the paintwork and prepared it for use as an Airbnb or longer-term rental. Now they were considering whether they should advertise it for rental or find someone of their choosing by word of mouth.

'Leave it with me, Bryn. I'm sure we can find something for you—even if it's only temporary.'

He gave her a small smile and pushed his chair back, clinging to it while he hoisted himself up and Sophie entered the room.

'Morning, Soph.' Ginny waved a hand toward Bryn. 'This is Bryn, one of our current guests. Bryn, Sophie, our soon-to-be son-in-law's sister.'

Sophie crossed the room and held out her undamaged arm. 'Nice to meet you.'

'Bit of an argument with a kangaroo, I hear.'

She grinned ruefully. 'Could say that. I came off better than he did though.'

'Hmm.' He shared a sympathetic smile with her. 'I'll be off then. Talk to you later, Ginny—and thanks again.'

'You're welcome.'

Bryn limped slowly to the veranda.

Filled with compassion, Ginny remained motionless as he left. Bryn was a pleasant, private soul who, apart from daily walks to the falls each day, had mostly kept to himself—only coming to the homestead each evening to collect his dinner then returning the dishes the following morning, washed, dried, and packed neatly on the tray. Despite his obvious injury, it struck Ginny that perhaps he had a secret to keep. Or perhaps his need for privacy was because he'd spent a long period in hospital and now valued the peace? Regardless, she would visit Andrew and ask not only about temporary accommodation for Bryn, but about the dreaded question that had plagued her since the overheard conversation outside the general store.

14

The following morning, Francene and Eleanor ate breakfast together in the gracious dining room with its solid timber furniture and pale walls hung with Featherwood Falls history. Francene's favourite was a picture of a horse-drawn carriage outside the Featherwood Station homestead with the backdrop of purple and green hills and peaks.

Gathering courage, Francene leaned closer to Eleanor. 'Could I ask your advice on something please?'

'Of course. Ask away.' Eleanor patted her mouth with the serviette and gave her full attention to the younger woman.

'If you were able to buy a home in a small town but it would take all the money you have and you didn't have a job, would you still take the gamble?'

Eleanor blinked. 'I guess it would depend on my age at the time—and of course whether the town felt like home. As I mentioned, I made a similar decision in coming here to live. People told me I was being silly—romanticising. But I know different. I may not have many years left, but what I have, I plan to enjoy.'

Francene could feel Eleanor's eyes burning into hers.

'Tell me more, Francene. This is about you, isn't it?'

She squirmed in her seat like an inquisitive child who'd asked a question they shouldn't have. 'Yes. Well, at least I'm thinking about it. I know I've only been here a few days, but I think I've fallen in love with the place.'

'And can you afford to live here without a job?'

Francene sighed. 'No. I guess I'm dreaming. That's the trouble with these little places, isn't it? There's not much available unless you want to pick seasonal fruit and vegetables or have something you can do online.'

'There's nothing wrong with that. Good, honest work hurt no one. But, Francene, you're obviously not straight out of school. You must have filled in a few years. I understand your desire for privacy, but perhaps if you'd share a little of your life with me, I could understand better—and help you.'

A sudden urge to get up and run away threatened her. Was she doing the right thing, sharing her life with this woman and hoping it wouldn't be bandied around the district like Chinese whispers? *Get a grip on yourself.* She cleared her throat.

'I'm thirty-five and was married for ten years—until my husband died. During that time, I worked as an administration officer in local government.'

Eleanor nodded. 'And before that? You mentioned your parents live in France and your sister in Perth. Was your husband the reason you stayed in Brisbane?'

Francene screwed up her face despairingly. 'I had a fabulous job. A pastry chef. I've always loved cooking, especially decorating cakes and making desserts. I did my apprenticeship and worked in the patisserie in Edward Street.'

'Oh! I used to buy a vanilla slice from there when I was in the area.' Eleanor beamed. 'We may have met before?'

Francene shrugged. 'Maybe.'

'What made you give it up to work in an office?' Eleanor's voice had softened, her stare becoming more intense.

Francene clenched her jaw. How much was she prepared to share? For a moment, she wished she'd bitten her tongue and said nothing. But intuition drove her on. This woman had shared more than the story of her life with Francene. She'd insisted on paying for Francene's hotel costs—"It's on me, dear," she'd said. "I invited you to come and you did, so the least I can do is cover the hotel costs for us both. That way I don't feel guilty about talking a pretty, young woman into travelling miles from home with a doddery old lady."

'My husband.' She fought back the anger that continued to brew whenever she reflected on how gullible she'd been. She had fallen for his charm and been willing to obey his every wish. *I was a fool.*

'Oh. Let me guess. He didn't like you leaving his warm bed at some ungodly hour of the morning and being so tired in the evenings that you fell asleep before eight o'clock?'

Francene chuckled, surprised at the older woman's perception. 'Got it in one.'

'Right. Well, let's forget about him and tell me more about what you would like to do if you were to buy a house in ... shall we say somewhere like Featherwood Falls?'

Knotting and unknotting her fingers together in her lap, Francene gabbled, 'Since I was a little girl, I've dreamed about owning a cottage. Something big enough to run a small tearoom and patisserie from—somewhere I could share my love of antique furniture and pretty knick-knacks with people, as well as delicious pastries and cakes. I even know what I'd call it.' She stopped. Had she said too much?

'Tea, Tarts and Treasures.'

They both giggled, Eleanor pressing her serviette to her eyes. 'Oh, that's priceless. I love it!'

Conspiratorially, she leaned toward Francene

again. 'Do you know what? I believe that's exactly what a small town like Featherwood Falls needs. Lola has serviced the morning and afternoon tea needs of passers-by for decades, but I know Ryan and Emma are not keen on following in Lola's footsteps—they have too much else on their plate with the post office and mail run, not to mention their new baby and Emma's piano teaching.' She paused, reflecting. 'I'm sure they will be happy to continue serving coffee and café-style lunches with the help of local staff, but there's definitely an opportunity for something more here.'

'What about this hotel?'

'Alex and Briony offer beautiful meals, but I believe they are far too busy to add more to their workload. Anyway, they have ideas of improvements they want to make here ... so "Tea, Tarts and Treasures" would be a perfect addition to this town.'

Francene's pulse raced. While unemployed and unable to borrow money for a home in Brisbane, she was sure she could scrape enough together to buy the house Pam had shown her. Her savings were all but gone, thanks to Kyle. Thankfully, he had forgotten about the life insurance policy she had taken out for each of them when they married and, until her work contract had run out, she had squirreled away every cent she could. Kyle's policy had been paid out following his death and soon after, a lump sum had been transferred to her account—the superannuation he had earned in the fifteen years he'd miraculously held his job as an architect. A pang of guilt heightened her heart rate further. With the loss of their own home and then the contract expiring at her workplace, she had reached the lowest ebb in her life. For days she had mentally wandered, lost and lonely, unable to move forward. Then the difficulty in obtaining a rental property had hit, so she had sold most of their furniture, put her belongings in storage, and decided to live as inexpensively as possible while she worked out what to do next.

This could be it!

The vision of a man with a walking stick, his handsome face pained and tired but wearing a beautiful smile, flashed before her eyes. Something had damaged him, but he was obviously striving to heal if the snippets shared by Alex and Briony were anything to go by. *If he can do it, then so can I.*

Reaching across the table, she squeezed Eleanor's hand. 'Thank you. I'm going to see if Briony and Alex have time for a quick chat, then I'm calling Pam to make an offer on that cottage.'

Before her confidence faded, she stood, gaining strength from Eleanor's smile, and strode toward the kitchen.

15

Two days. That's all he had left before he had to vacate the cabin to allow other visitors to stay.

Bryn had done his laundry that morning, making use of Ginny's generous offer for him to use the washing machine in the old-fashioned stone-brick room near the back door of the homestead. Now his jeans and shirts flapped on the line while he added to his growing pile of carved birds. While his hands shaped and smoothed the wood, his mind drifted to the girl—or rather, woman, he corrected himself—he'd met in the store. Francene. Even her name was pretty, while her seeming desire for anonymity and privacy intrigued him. Was she also suffering somehow? Perhaps her problem was a less visible one than his. A frown crept onto his forehead. She'd caught his gaze and dived behind the shelving as if trying to avoid him. Yet she was friendly and polite to Lola—at least that was the way he'd seen it. Perhaps she was frightened of something—or someone. A man.

He paused, lifting his head to follow the *clip-clop* sound of a horse approaching.

The brisk march of the bay mare halted metres from him, and Ginny called out, 'Hey, Bryn. I've got some good news for you.'

He put his project down and stood, pausing for a few seconds and waiting for the pain in his hip to settle. Then he ambled toward her and lay a confident hand on the mare's neck. 'Nice horse.'

'This is Akela. We've had her for years now, so she's no youngster—but I love riding her and, as you can see from her round belly, she could do with more exercise than she's currently getting.' Her gaze settled on him. 'You're a horseman?'

He shrugged. 'Long time ago. I love horses though. Did a bit of campdrafting and cutting. What is this news you've got for me?'

'You know the place on the left-hand side of the road heading from here back into town?'

'Yeah—the one with the old oak tree in the front garden?'

'That's it. It used to be Kirk's, but recently he sold it to Claire and Rhys. They can't move into it until sometime next year when the new police officer arrives, but

I talked to them and they said if you'd like to stay there until they need it, you're welcome.'

Bryn straightened as the words sunk in. 'Really?'

'If you're interested, I said you'd pop up to our house and talk to Claire. She's in her office around the back, but she and Sophie will head into town after lunch. If it's not what you want, I'm on my way to visit my nephew next door, so will ask him about the workers' accommodation on Glenrowan.'

'Thanks, Ginny. Claire's place sounds awesome. I noticed the shed out the back too, which will be fantastic—if I'm allowed to use it.'

Ginny smiled, urging the horse to move forward. 'I'm sure the shed is included. Catch you later.'

The horse trotted smartly along the track; Bryn's eyes glued to its departing rump. Then he hurried to the cabin, grabbed his hat and walking stick from the veranda, and headed up the rise to the homestead.

FOLLOWING the pavers past the line where his washing flapped, he arrived at a set of stone steps leading up to French doors. Through the glass, Claire sat in front of a large computer screen, her face scrunched in concentration.

He knocked, and her head lifted. She got up and opened the door.

'Gidday, Bryn.' With a wry grin, she added, 'I bet Mum's just talked to you about our house?'

'She has. Have I come at a bad time?'

'No. Come in. I was about to make myself a coffee. Would you like one?'

'Thanks. Sounds great.'

He followed her through the room, admiring the clever way the side veranda had been converted to a light and colourful studio. An attached bedroom and wide hallway led to the kitchen-living area he had sat in before.

'Grab a seat. How do you like your coffee?'

'Umm. White, no sugar, thanks.'

'Flat white okay?'

'Perfect.'

For a few minutes he perched on a chair at the table while the coffee machine ground the beans and the steam wand sizzled and spat. Then Claire placed a large mug of the fragrant steaming drink in front of him and sat opposite. His eyes met hers as he sipped his coffee.

'How long are you thinking of staying?' Claire asked.

He took a deep breath and released it slowly. 'Good question, but one I'm sorry I can't answer.'

'So ... two, three months?'

'Yeah. For a start, anyway.'

'I don't mean to pry, but where do you call home?'

'I grew up on the family farm near Armidale, if that's what you mean?'

'And you don't want to go back?'

He shook his head firmly. 'No. My elder brother and dad run the place. No room for anyone else ... at this stage anyway. I've got another brother who's keen to farm but he's up north working in the fishing industry. I've promised Mum I'll drive down for Christmas, but as for anything else—I guess time will tell.'

Neither of them spoke for a few long seconds.

'Families eh?' Claire said.

'Yeah. I've been away over twenty years now and done a lot of other stuff—some enjoyable and some not so much.' He took a gulp of coffee, relishing the hot liquid running down his dry throat. She hadn't asked outright, but he could feel her interest and for some reason he didn't find it nosy. 'I've spent the past two years recovering from an accident.'

'I gathered that. Car?'

'No. Fell off a roof.'

'Good grief!'

'Yeah. Not recommended.'

'How did it happen?'

'I was working for a roofing company. We had the contract with a home-building mob in a new housing estate. I'm still not sure what happened, but I was on the roof and my mate was beside me passing the iron sheets. The last thing I remember was a gust of wind catching one of them. I must have stepped back and next thing I was waking up in hospital.'

'Geez. You're lucky to be alive!'

'Yeah. Believe me, there were plenty of times I wished I wasn't.'

'So what injuries are you recovering from?'

'Broken back, smashed pelvis and hip. Could have been worse—have to be thankful I'm not in a wheelchair.'

'I guess so. Still, I can understand why you're looking for a change of lifestyle.'

He chuckled. 'You're not wrong. Luckily, I get a government allowance while I'm not able to work, so it doesn't really matter where I live.'

'How will you fill your days?'

'I enjoy woodcarving and making handmade furniture—hence the idea of a shed where I can be creative and not mess up the house.'

'Sounds good. We haven't had much time to get to know one another, but perhaps we could do a contract for three months and by then we'll both know where we stand and what the future holds for you. And Rhys and I.'

'Would I be able to have a look at the place?'

'Of course. It's still furnished because Kirk only needed his everyday things when he moved in here.'

'Can I rent the furniture? I don't have any of my own.' He swallowed a breath. Would Claire think he was a loser because he had so little? 'I've been living with my sister in Brisbane while having treatment.'

If she'd had any doubts about him, they weren't evident. Bryn's hopes rose again.

'Perfect. I was wondering what we would do with it all. One of these days we'll move in ourselves and probably keep most of it—Kirk lived pretty simply, so there's only the basics.'

'Sounds good.'

Claire rose and collected the mugs. 'If you can give me half an hour to finish the job I'm working on, we can nip down and I'll show you through.'

A burst of happiness filled his chest—a lightness he hadn't felt in a long, long time.

THEY DROVE onto the gravel strip leading from the road along the side of the house and ending in front of a large shed. Almost as big as the cottage, one side of the interior was clearly designated for vehicles, while the other half comprised a wooden floor, a work-bench, and shelving running along the back. A dividing wall separated the workshop from the car shed.

'Kirk renovated this when he moved in because, like you, he enjoys making things. He said the changes he made kept the winter chill out as well as a lot of dust. Now the welder and everything else he needs has been moved up to the farm.'

A cow mooed close by, and Claire laughed when Bryn jumped. 'Sorry. Should have warned you. That's Buttons. This place has quite a few acres with it and some of our hand-reared cows live here. They keep it tidy and are easy to handle in the little wooden yards over in the corner if we need to check or medicate them.'

They wandered the few metres to the fence where Buttons was staring intently at them both.

Claire reached out and rubbed the cow's face, cautiously avoiding the electric wire that ran along the top, ensuring the cow's neck didn't crush the fence in an attempt to munch on the grass inside the yard.

'No hay today, girl. You've got plenty to eat in that paddock.' She turned to Bryn. 'Come on. We'll have a quick look through the house then I'd better get back to the office for a little while. Sophie's grooming the horses—one-handed—but when she's finished, I'll drop her at the hotel so she and Briony can visit Sam. She also wants to reassure her brother she'll make a full recovery and not ruin their wedding.'

Bryn lifted his eyebrows as he followed her through the small timber gate dividing the house plot from the shed and outer yard. Beside the porch was a laundry containing old-fashioned concrete tubs and a well-used washing machine.

Claire waved a hand toward it as they trod the two steps leading onto the porch. 'Laundry, obviously.' She unlocked the door, and they stepped inside.

Bryn blinked. 'Wow. This is really nice. I guess I was expecting an older-style kitchen that matched the age of the house.'

'That was the case when Kirk bought the place a few years ago, but he did a lot of work to it when he moved in. New kitchen and bathroom, painted right through, as well as outside—and opened up the front veranda again. It had been closed off years earlier with horrible sliding windows and cheap wood.'

He followed her through the central hallway, trying unsuccessfully to contain his delight as he glanced left and right. By the time they stepped out on the east-facing front veranda, he was buzzing with anticipation.

'When can I move in?'

She grinned. 'Now's fine with me.'

He held out his hand.

As she took it and they exchanged a mutual nod, Bryn's hopes soared. *Perhaps this is the new start I've been waiting for.*

16

Akela trotted along the grass verge beside Glenrowan's driveway, snorting occasionally at a bird flying out of the bushes, hesitant and requiring Ginny's firm voice and leg—as though she too remembered the ride she and Ginny had made over four years earlier.

Ginny gritted her teeth, determined to put the event from her mind. But no matter how strong she was, the memories of that day flooded back. It had simply been an opportunity to talk to her neighbour about haymaking while exercising Akela at the same time. Instead, the journey had resulted in finding the evidence that put her husband's murderer behind bars.

This time, she was greeted by her cheery nephew, the current manager of the property and a young man she loved as dearly as her own children.

'Hey, Auntie Ginny. How's things?'

He held Akela by the reins while Ginny slid down her side, then tied the mare to the fence with calm, practiced hands.

They hugged before Andrew waved toward the house. 'Cold drink?'

'Yes please.'

'Akela's looking good. Been in a good paddock.'

They both laughed as Ginny glanced at her own disappearing waistline. 'We both have.'

She followed him inside, casting a cursory look around. Although dated and wearing evidence of a bachelor's pad rather than a family home, the house was clean, the lawns and driveway neatly mowed, and the waft of fresh-brewed coffee scented the air.

Andrew's lanky frame towered above her as they entered the kitchen.

He withdrew two glasses from the cupboard and filled them with iced water from the fridge, then lifted the kettle. 'Tea or coffee?'

'I'll have coffee, thanks.'

For a few minutes, they chatted about family issues —how Sarah, Andrew's mother, was enjoying her new home in Warwick, where Briony was at with their wedding plans, and Sophie and Sam's accident.

'They were lucky,' Ginny said. 'Well—as lucky as anyone can be after an accident as bad as theirs. Sophie was a bit subdued this morning. No doubt the aftermath of the whole thing, her concern for Sam, and finding aches in places she didn't know she had has caught up with her.'

'I bet. Poor girl.'

'Claire's taking her to the hotel after lunch so she and Briony can visit Sam in the hospital. Then they were going to run through wedding stuff—I suspect as much to keep Sophie's mind on something other than the accident than for any other reason.'

'And you?' Andrew asked.

Ginny smiled, her eyes locking with his. Grey eyes and sandy coloured hair, Andrew was almost as familiar to her as Lyndon had been.

'I'm good—and you might as well know before you hear it from someone else, Kirk and I are now married.'

He gave a sheepish grin and put his hand over hers. 'I know—and I'm delighted. Don't blame you for eloping either.'

'We didn't elope! We were simply finding out what was required for a courthouse ceremony and ... well, everything happened at once. Neither of us wanted any fuss.' She shrugged. 'Anyway, it's done now and we can focus on Alex and Briony's big day.'

'I get it. Can't promise that a bit of celebration won't happen though—you know your girls. No need for an excuse to have a party.'

'Well, if something is organised—and I'm not

saying I want it to be—as long as I don't have to do anything, I won't object.'

'Good.'

They finished their coffee in silence before Andrew narrowed his eyes and focused on Ginny's face.

'You've got something you want to talk about, haven't you?'

Ginny refused to look at him for a long minute, clasping both hands around her mug as though it would save her from peril. 'I recently overheard a couple of your pickers talking outside Lola's shop.'

'And ...'

'They mentioned the possibility of your position here being terminated.'

He leaned back in his chair, his hands clasped behind his head and laughed. 'Good old bush telegraph. Mostly gets it right, but you can count on someone mucking up the facts.'

'So it's not true then?'

His face morphed into a serious, worried expression, aging him beyond his twenty-eight years. 'Not exactly. But I suspect what you also heard but are not prepared to voice is that Nigel Ward is eligible to apply for parole at the end of this year—and I can assure you that no one is happy about that, especially me.'

The news slugged her with the same ferocity a lump of wood might have had it fallen on her. Slumped in her chair, every whisper of strength drained from her body. She bowed her head, desperate to hide her emotions from her insightful nephew, and drew some regular breaths before facing him again.

'Do you think it will be successful? The parole application, I mean.'

He rolled his eyes. 'You know how weak our justice system is. Of course he'll get it. Mum has contacts and we're working on a plan if he is released—and before you ask, no, it has absolutely nothing to do with my father and never will. As far as Mum and I are concerned, my father's crimes are way more serious. No one knows how many lives he's responsible for ending. The worst part is we're his family. So ignoring him is okay while he's inside, but one day we'll be discussing the same worry we are now—that a person we wish we had never met might be right here in this kitchen where we're sitting.'

Ginny couldn't hold back the tears any longer. They carved silent trails down her cheeks. Moving closer, Andrew wrapped his arms around her as the sobs broke free, muting the song of the magpies outside.

17

———

'Knock, knock,' Francene said as she stood in the kitchen doorway of the hotel. 'Have you got a minute to talk?'

'Aye. If you don't mind chatting here—I've got a couple of things on the go and I can't leave them,' Alex said.

She glanced to where he was chopping a pile of what looked to her like ingredients for a Thai-style soup while intermittently stirring a pot of fragrant-smelling liquid.

'Of course.' She moved closer, pressing her hands against the edge of the bench.

'Something on your mind?'

'Is Briony here? It would be nice to talk to you both.'

'Sorry. She and Sophie have gone to Warwick to

visit Sam. You can save it until later if you like—or fire away and I'll try to help?'

He shot her a grin, and she smiled back.

'Do you think another food outlet would fit into this village without taking from the store ... or you?'

The knife paused, resting on the chopping board. 'I guess it would depend on what sort of facility you are talking about.' His eyes narrowed as they met hers, and her stomach did an anxious flip. 'Is this business something you're thinking of—I mean for you to operate?'

'Y-yes.' She drew a long breath, kicking herself internally for raising the subject. It was a stupid idea in such a small place and the last thing she wanted was to be ostracised by a community she was feeling so comfortable in.

'Look, don't worry. I can see you're busy and I'm just dreaming.' She stepped back from the bench, clamped her mouth shut, and turned to leave.

'Hang on a tick. You've just got my interest and now you're leaving? Come back and tell me more.'

She pivoted, the edges of her mouth twitching as she decided whether to say something or to keep them firmly closed. Giving in, she took a breath before responding.

'I'm thinking about staying here in Featherwood Falls.'

'Well, that's a good start. You've obviously got some

experience in the kitchen, and I could always do with a hand if you're looking for work.'

Her shoulders slumped in relief, and she smiled. 'Thank you. There's a house along the road a bit, between here and the store that's for sale. It's kinda cute and I was thinking it would make a nice tearoom.'

'You mean like an old-fashioned style of café?' He stirred the pot again and reduced the heat before giving her his full attention.

'I guess so. I'd like to get back into baking pastries and cakes, and I thought that as this hotel mainly caters for people who want a main meal, and the general store has a fast-food takeaway menu, that perhaps a nice tea house where couples passing through could stop and have morning or afternoon tea —or even high tea for special occasions—might be a good alternative. While they're here, they could browse through the gift shelves where I'd like to stock items that blend with country living and perhaps quirky little things that are often hard to find.' She stopped, suddenly aware that she'd barely paused for breath and Alex was staring at her wide eyed.

Pressing her palms together, she entangled her fingers and pushed her thumbs against her face. 'So ... what do you think? Is it something that might work?'

Alex rubbed a hand over the auburn stubble on his chin and raised his eyebrows. 'I do. I haven't lived here very long myself, but I know how quickly our business has grown and …' He turned and waved a sweeping arm. 'You can see how much there is to do. Even with Briony and our staff, we often struggle to keep up with demand, especially on Friday and Saturday nights.'

A flush of hope trickled through her. 'So you wouldn't have any objections if I was to start up a business?'

'Not at all. And better than that—while you're getting yourself established, I'd love for you to come and work for us in your spare time.'

'Really?' Her voice squeaked with incredulity.

'Yes. In the next few weeks, we've not only got our own wedding to get through, but our friends Ashleigh and Damian are getting married on New Year's Eve. Although they're having the service and reception at Kallala—that's an enormous home and gardens up a side road between Warwick and here—we've been asked to do the catering.' He gave a vague nod toward the storeroom off the kitchen. 'It'll be a fairly simple menu and I've already made a start on a few things, but they want me to do petit fours for dessert and the wedding cake.' He grimaced. 'I could do with a hand for them.'

Francene nodded enthusiastically. 'I'd love to help.'

As she withdrew into her own thoughts, visualising herself wearing the uniform she'd kept hidden in the back of her wardrobe since Kyle had convinced her to resign from the patisserie, Lola's welcoming face flashed through her mind.

'What about Lola and her family? Do you think they would mind me starting something so close to their own business?'

He shook his head. 'I doubt it, but it might be a good idea to have the conversation with them. Lola and Frank are supposed to be retired. Tricky when you live on the premises. But Ryan and a couple of local women are gradually reshaping things to suit both the community and them, which will probably change Lola's baking schedule too.'

'Okay. I'll talk to them before I ring the real estate agent. Thanks heaps. You've been a great help.'

Grinning, he turned back to the pile of vegetables. 'You're welcome—and if you'd like to start work now, you're welcome to that too.'

She hesitated, unsure if he was serious. 'Would you mind if I had the conversation with Lola and Frank first? If they're not happy and I can't buy the house, then there's probably no point in me staying here. I'll have to go back to Brisbane and look for work.'

His eyes fastened on hers, his face softening as though he could read her dread of having to return to the noise and bustle of the city and the anxiety welling within her.

'You'll be fine. I reckon you belong here as much as I do.'

18

---

*H*alf an hour later, she approached the store, intrigued to find Frank—Lola's thin, wiry husband—hammering a timber frame in the small alcove between the post office and shop.

'Hello there!' he called.

She stared at the old man with his wide-brimmed hat shading his eyes and a leather pouch strapped to his waist.

'Hi.'

He grinned, inclining his head toward the frame. 'I believe you're the one responsible for this.'

'Me?' she squeaked, frowning. 'Sorry?'

'Don't worry, love. I mean it in good faith. Apparently, you asked Lola about a book exchange?'

She nodded mutely.

'Good thing as it turns out. We've been meaning

to get something built for years, but with the shop and post office keeping us busy before Ryan came home—and then the baby coming along—it was one of those jobs that kept being put away for another time.'

Francene released a relieved whoosh of breath. 'Oh, I see what you mean.' She pointed to the pile of timber on the ground. 'So you're building a book exchange here?'

'Yep. Won't be big—just filling in this space will restrict how much it will hold ... but I reckon it'll be somewhere people will stop and browse when they come to buy bread or collect their mail. What do you think?'

'It will be perfect. And if I'm still around, I'll be the first to borrow—and to drop off a few I've finished reading.'

He narrowed his eyes. 'Thinking of heading back to the big smoke then?'

'Actually, that's what I'm here for—' She paused, forcing away the thread of anxiety worming its way through her insides. 'I wondered if I could talk to you and Lola about ... something.'

'Sure. Time for a cuppa anyway. Why don't you head into the shop and give Lola a cooee. I'll pack up these tools and be in shortly.'

She gave a quick smile of acknowledgement and walked the few steps to the shop door.

Janet greeted her cheerily. 'Gidday, Francene. Time to stock up on a few treats?'

'Not today thanks, Janet. I'd like to have a quick chat with Lola. Is she here?'

'Out the back. She's minding the little fellow while Ryan's doing the mail run and Emma's teaching piano. Hang on, I'll get her for you.'

The woman disappeared through the back door while Francene hovered, taking the opportunity to have a closer look at the menu listed on the blackboard and the items resting on plates in the glass-fronted cabinet. Lamingtons, scones, a large chocolate cake, and a few pre-packaged gluten-free biscuits in an airtight jar. *Nothing I can't improve on—or need to compete with.*

The adjoining door between the kitchen and the house swung open, and Lola emerged with a baby on her hip and with Janet close behind her.

'Gidday, love. How's your holiday going?'

Francene smiled. *Is that what the locals call it? I suppose having nothing to do except wander around a small country town is close enough.* 'Pretty good thanks. Umm ...' She glanced at Janet before meeting Lola's eyes. 'Could I have a quiet chat with you and your husband?'

Lola raised an eyebrow as Frank burst through the front door, sending the tiny bell into a frantic jingle. 'Sure, love. Here's the man himself. Shall we go through to the side veranda?'

Taking the hint, Janet retreated to the grocery shelves and proceeded to unpack a crate of bread loaves while the baby and Francene studied each other in silence.

She'd had little to do with babies—mostly only admiring the new offspring of one of her office comrades or dutifully offering passing comments on how cute the child was and asking politely how the mother was getting on being at home all day.

This time though, the twinkling blue eyes and chubby face broke into a smile before the baby chortled excitedly, and Francene smiled back, unable to stem the surge of love that pulsed through her.

'This is Liam,' Lola said. 'He's our grandson—Ryan and Emma's little fellow. Emma teaches music two mornings a week—and on Saturdays for those who work or are at school, so we get to have lots of time with this precious, wee fellow.'

Francene's hopes rose a notch higher. If Lola was busy minding Liam, surely she would welcome a suggestion that might reduce the time she had to spend in the shop.

Under the shade of the veranda, the three adults shuffled around one of the small tables with the baby sitting on Lola's lap and waving a spoon wildly around. There was only one other person—a man in the opposite corner who appeared to be about to leave. He stood unsteadily, folded his newspaper, and tucked it under his arm before removing the battered hat from the table where it had been sitting next to a large, empty mug.

'See you folks next time.'

'Thanks, Bill,' Lola said.

'Sure will,' Frank added.

They waited a minute while he shuffled out, allowing the baby to distract them as he flung the spoon on the floor.

Frank picked it up and exchanged it for the baby toy Lola magically produced from her apron pocket.

'Righto. While this little fellow is busy, how can we help you, love?' Lola said.

Francene drew a deep breath. 'I-I'm interested in buying the house—the cottage—up the road with the "For Sale" sign in front of it.'

'Lovely!' Lola exclaimed without waiting for more information.

Francene smiled. 'You might not think so once you've heard what I'd like to do with it.'

She now had the full attention of both Lola and Frank.

'I've had a talk with Alex—at the pub—and he's happy with my plans.'

'Which are?' Frank asked.

'Turning it in to a tearoom-come-little-gift-store.'

Lola straightened, her eyes wide. 'Well ... that

sounds lovely.' She touched the back of her hand against Frank's arm. 'Don't you reckon?'

Nodding, he swung his gaze from his wife to Francene again. 'And you're worried we might put in an objection to the material change of use?'

'Yes, I guess so.'

'Well, I'm telling you now, you'll have no worries from us,' Frank said. 'For decades. this town has only had this store or the pub for locals and those who pass through to buy food of any sort from. But as you can see, the menu is pretty basic, and Lola and I are no longer in our youth. So ... if it's our blessing you're looking for, you've got it and I doubt you'll have any problems with council either. We have one of the councillors living here in Featherwood Falls now, and I know he and his wife will love it. They're the morning-coffee-in-the-café type but I'm sure they only come here because there's nowhere else—and of course they can't resist one of Lola's lamingtons,' he finished with a chuckle.

'It will be a load off my shoulders to no longer have to worry about who's going to make the lamingtons if I can't—and anyway, there's plenty of room in this town for more options. You can see from all the new houses going up, it's a growing community and I'm sure anyone who attempts to bring a bit of old-fashioned hospitality to town will be welcome.' Lola glanced down at the baby, who seemed perfectly happy chomping on his toy while one tiny hand plucked at the flowers on Lola's apron. 'A tearoom, you say. Please, tell us more?'

Francene's cheeks flushed bright pink and she leaned forward to share her ideas. 'I have a few pieces of antique furniture stored in Brisbane, and my grandmother's old china and bits and pieces I've accumulated since my parents moved overseas. I'm also a qualified pastry chef—one with a dream to one day open my own café.' She stopped for a second, considering how much she needed to share.

'Keep going,' Lola urged.

'As soon as I saw the cottage, I could visualise it coming to life with little cloth-covered tables on the veranda and in one of the inside rooms. With gift items stored on dresser shelves and an updated kitchen, I believe it would add a nice stopover for passers-by as well. Only ... I don't want to step on toes or upset anyone already in the catering business here. As I said, I haven't talked to Briony yet, but Alex was quite enthusiastic—he even offered me a job to help at the pub part-time until I get started.'

'Well, there you are. You have our blessing, Francene. And I can assure you competition is a good thing, even when it's not really because our venues will be catering for customers' differing needs.' Lola laughed, and both Frank and Francene couldn't help but join in.

Francene felt as though she was walking on air as she glided back to the hotel minutes later. As she pounded up the stairs to her room, she returned to reality with a thud. What if someone has already put in an offer for the house? With fingers crossed and her heart thumping in her chest, she dialled Pam's number.

19

Ginny slumped in the saddle on the way home, relieved that, like her, Akela was in no hurry, allowing time for Ginny to digest her thoughts.

It was true. Nigel Ward would return to Glenrowan within a month or two, not in several years' time as the court had originally decreed. His return would most likely displace Andrew as manager of Glenrowan and bring a level of anxiety to Featherwood Station. It was inevitable that he would return to his home at some point—but Ginny had tucked that thought into the recesses of her mind, hoping something would change before that day arrived.

Akela startled as a wallaby hopped out of the bushes nearby, jerking Ginny's attention to the present. She longed for Kirk's solid comfort.

Oh, Kirk. Your little mining venture? Will Nigel cause problems for you too?

Too drained to shed another tear, Ginny let her mind wander back over the past four years.

Kirk's discovery of minerals in the abandoned mines deep in the rugged hills behind Featherwood Station had brought confirmation from the Department of Resources that the minerals were pure. That finding explained Nigel's desperation to buy the land and the reason he had killed Lyndon, and subsequently ended up in prison, when Lyndon refused to sell it.

Until now, the difficulty in extracting the ore had dismissed any interest from other parties, and Kirk's licence allowed him to remove tiny chips of silver, lead, and zinc from the rocks unimpeded by competition from both mining conglomerates and other locals. The occasional piece of gold, no bigger than a fingernail, had been a delightful secret discovery that only Kirk and Ginny shared—and had been squirrelled away in Kirk's hiding place until he had enough to make the journey to the dealer in Brisbane worthwhile. It was the proceeds from Kirk's hobby that had helped him invest in Featherwood Station, cementing the business and emotional bond he, Ginny, and her daughters now shared.

With the stables in sight, Akela broke into a trot, jolting Ginny to the present once again. In the distance, the big green tractor circled one of the lucerne paddocks, the sound of its powerful engine and the regular clunk of the mower-conditioner blown toward her by the hot summer breeze.

While gulping deep breaths, she focused on the horse, perspiration trickling down Ginny's face and back as they reached the stables. After dismounting, she swapped her riding helmet for her wide-brimmed Akubra, unsaddled Akela and hosed her down, barely noticing the spray that splashed back over her own body. A brisk rub-down and a small tin of horse pellets satisfied the mare's requirements before Ginny released her into the paddock, then turned and strode toward the new all-terrain farm vehicle, referred to as the ATV.

Within minutes, she pulled up at the gate to the lucerne paddock, got out of the vehicle, and waved to Kirk. The tractor quietened and he climbed down the steps.

Despite the fifty metres separating them, his delighted smile sent a familiar tremor of love and excitement through her. She quickened her pace, desperate to feel his arms around her.

'Hey there.' He wrapped her in a hug, giving a gruff chortle. 'This is a pleasant welcome—especially since it's only been a couple of hours.'

'I know. I've just had some bad news though—and I need to tell you.'

Frowning, he held her at arm's length. 'You've got me. You know I'll always be here for you.'

She nodded, swallowing the lump in her throat, and pointed to the tractor. 'It's too hot to stand out here and talk. Let's sit in the cab.'

In silence, he held her hand as they walked to the tractor before hauling himself up the steps behind her.

With the air-conditioning rapidly cooling the confined area, Ginny shared the conversation she'd had with Andrew an hour earlier. When she finished, he sat back in the seat, stroking his grey-speckled beard with long, work-worn fingers.

'We knew it had to happen. No point worrying about it yet though. Who knows, he might come out a changed man and be the neighbour his parents always were.'

'Do leopards really change their spots?'

He took her face between his hands. 'Sweetheart, we've got so much happening here at the moment, there's no point getting stressed over it—at least not until we know for certain he's returning to Glenrowan. Let's give him a chance. Killing Lyndon was not premeditated—at least not according to the court— and I'm sure he's regretted his actions. Every day in that prison would have reminded him of that.'

She huffed. 'You really believe he'll return a changed man?'

He shrugged. 'I hope so—and I'd like to think he'll have a completely different attitude.'

You're such a good person.

They shared a small smile.

'Shall I finish cutting this paddock now? Or would you like me to come up to the house with you?'

'I'll be okay, but thanks.'

'How about we go to the pub for dinner tonight?'

'That's a lovely thought, but I need a while to think things over. Tomorrow instead? It's Friday, so there'll be the usual crowd which will be nice.' She grimaced. 'What's the bet the news has already filtered into the community and there are others who have the same concerns as me? I've no doubt his return will be the talk of the town for a while.'

Kirk hugged her again. 'I know.'

She climbed down and jumped from the bottom step before looking back up at him. 'See you soon?'

'Yeah. Another few rounds then I'll be back at the house and we can talk some more.' His kind face crinkled with love and sympathy.

She grinned up at him, her heart melting, then made her way back to the ATV.

SHE HAD ALMOST REACHED the farm-stay cabins when Bryn stepped onto the track and waved. Slowing, she pulled closer to him and switched off the vehicle. 'Gidday, Bryn. Everything alright?'

'Hi, Ginny. I thought I'd pass on the good news before Claire beats me to it.'

Raising her eyebrows at his wide grin, Ginny waited.

'I'm moving into the house down the road.'

In an instant, a flood of guilt flowed through her. She had intended asking Andrew about a spare cabin or caravan and the subject had completely slipped her mind. 'Fabulous. That's a great outcome for you, Bryn.'

'Yeah. It might not be for long, but I'm happy about that. Gives me a couple of months to think about things ...' He lifted his stiff leg. '... and get this thing working properly.'

'You don't think you'll get bored living out here?'

He shook his head firmly. 'No way. It's a beautiful place, and I'll be able to get started on a project I've wanted to do for a while now.'

'Which is?'

'Woodwork. I don't mean just whittling the little birds. I'd like to get a few bigger pieces of wood and make some furniture.'

'Sounds interesting. There's plenty of timber on Featherwood Station if you'd like to make use of it. I'll speak to Kirk and perhaps the two of you could take the tractor up to the bush and have a look for a few felled branches to get you started.'

A stunned, wide-eyed expression filled Bryn's face, encouraging a smile from Ginny. 'Okay?'

'It's more than okay. I'm truly grateful—can't wait! Claire has given me the key to the house and said I can move in today. I hope that doesn't inconvenience you—with Dandelion Cottage, I mean.'

Ginny shook her head. 'Not at all. The new couple won't be here until after lunch on Saturday, so that gives me all day tomorrow to prepare for them. Lavender Cottage is ready for its guests whenever they arrive.' Her face softened in a grateful smile. 'Actually, you're helping me out by giving me more time to prepare for the next lot of guests.'

'Well, that's good then.' He stepped back as though preparing to retreat.

'Why don't you join us for dinner at the pub tomorrow night?' Ginny said. 'It's always busy on a Friday but it's an excellent opportunity for you to meet a few of the locals.'

Bryn gave her a measured look—a startled expression in his eyes as if she had just invited him to join them on a trek through Mongolia.

'Sure. Sounds good. Thanks.'

'We'll pick you up if you like. Saves fuel and gives you a chance to have a drink without worrying about our fearsome local cop picking you up for DUI.'

They both laughed before Ginny engaged the throttle and waved goodbye.

A warm sense of satisfaction blossomed within her, erasing much of the anxiety she'd felt only minutes earlier.

Perhaps having another nice guy around will help balance any problems Nigel sends our way. She crossed her fingers.

20

Bryn couldn't wipe the smile off his face as he packed his belongings and stowed them in his ute. The key to the new house jingled in his pocket and within half an hour, he was driving out of the Featherwood Station property, the chimney of his new abode rising above the hedge only a few hundred metres away.

After dragging out a box that had remained in his vehicle since leaving Brisbane, he fished out the neatly folded sheets, doona, and pile of towels and other essentials Mae had insisted he pack—"Just in case you find somewhere you want to stay awhile that doesn't supply linen". She had been right. The bed looked surprisingly comfortable, so he presumed Kirk hadn't needed it when he moved in with Ginny. He would drive into Stanthorpe or Warwick to purchase food and other items, but he figured he had all he needed for the first night at least—somewhere he could call home, even if only for three months.

And who knows what will happen between now and then.

Investigating the shed came next. Opening and shutting the cupboard doors, he then stored his precious tools before picking up the dusty broom propped in the corner and thoroughly sweeping the wooden floor. By the time he had removed cobwebs and wiped down the workbenches, his back and leg ached, his pulse raced, and his soul was filled with hopeful anticipation.

FRANCENE HOVERED OUTSIDE THE COTTAGE, her stomach churning.

In the narrow driveway, Pam parked her car in the shade of a large jacaranda tree, the last of its blue petals providing a carpet beneath the little red hatchback.

'Hello!' Pam called as she alighted the vehicle and hurried toward Francene. Under her arm was a red folder with the company's logo on the front and she held up a set of keys attached to a bright red plastic label. 'Are you ready?'

Francene nodded in silence, unable to speak for nervous exhilaration.

Pam unlocked the door and Francene followed her inside. 'I thought we'd sit at what will soon be your kitchen table and go through everything.'

'Thank you,' Francene whispered. Casting a glance around, the fizz of excitement escalated. Although having committed the interior to memory, there were little things she had missed on her first visit—the beautiful casement windows, French doors opening from the lounge onto the veranda, and the small empty room to the right of the front door taking up that corner of the veranda. *Perfect for storage.*

'Now,' Pam waved a document in the air, 'I received acceptance of your offer from the sellers and advice from your bank that you are indeed a cash buyer. So now we just have to get your signature on everything, confirm the settlement date, and in seven days' time, I can legally hand these keys over to you.'

'Wonderful,' Francene breathed.

They leaned over the table, with Pam flipping pages indicating where the next signature or initials needed to go and Francene following her instructions. When the documentation was complete, they both sat back and shared a smile.

'Happy?'

Francene nodded. 'Yes—and a little shocked.'

Pam tilted her head. 'Because they accepted your offer? Or because it's your first house?'

'It's not though,' she began. Then she clammed up, mentally punishing herself for being caught out. 'I mean, it's not my first house.'

'Oh, I thought you said you didn't have any real-estate capital—that the proceeds for this cottage resulted from an inheritance?'

Francene's shoulders sagged. What could she say that wouldn't bring back the terrifying memories she struggled so hard to suppress? Was it any of Pam's business anyway? She stared at the woman for a few long seconds, reading the genuine concern in Pam's voice. Guessing that she was in the mid-fifties region, her thoughts flew to her own mother. If she lived closer, there would be no way she would have been able to hide the truth from her. Except for the bank, not one other soul knew how much she had in her account or how much her deceased husband had squandered in gambling—accruing debts that had ensured the repossession of their home soon after he died. It had taken months to sort out, swallowing all that was left in their joint account and including ten thousand dollars of the insurance payout when it finally arrived. Suddenly, hiding the truth from everyone no longer seemed important.

'Yes.' She lifted her chin. 'What I have invested here is what was paid to me after my husband's death—

insurance and superannuation. I do not owe anyone anything and have a small nest egg left to set up my business—which is what I plan to do.'

Pam reached out a hand and placed it over Francene's. 'You're a strong woman and I can see you have determination. You will go far and as soon as you are set up for trading, I will be one of your first customers.'

'Thank you.' Relieved of an enormous burden and grateful Pam couldn't see the sudden panic circling within her, Francene smiled.

'Perfect. Now, to celebrate, why don't we have a coffee over at Lola's store—or better still, let's have lunch at the pub.'

'Sounds good.'

Leaving the car parked under the tree, they strolled along the road and entered the bar.

'Hello, ladies,' Briony said. 'How did it go—are you about to become one of Featherwood Falls' permanent residents?'

'Hi, Briony.' Francene beamed. 'I am, actually. In one week's time.'

'Ooh, that's fantastic news. Does Eleanor know?'

'What should Eleanor know? She's not deaf—yet.' Eleanor's perfect diction reached them, and all eyes swivelled to greet the elegant octogenarian as she crossed the room.

'Hi, Eleanor,' Francene said. 'It's all organised. In seven days' time I will be the new owner of the cottage up the road—and as soon as possible after that, I will open Featherwood Falls' very own "Tea, Tarts and Treasures".'

Throwing her arms wide, Eleanor gave Francene an unexpected hug, immediately followed by Briony and then Alex, who had entered the bar in time to hear Francene's announcement.

'I believe we need a drink to celebrate and then we'll go through to the dining room for lunch. Agreed?' Eleanor said, and heads nodded.

Pam, Eleanor, Francene, and Briony settled around a small table in the dining room, each with a glass of wine in front of them.

'I guess you'll have to return to Brisbane to arrange for your things to be shifted here, Francene,' Briony said.

'Yes, I will. Eleanor, what are your plans?'

'I suggest we both return on Sunday. I have a couple of appointments to attend and then will return this time next week for Briony and Alex's wedding. My house won't be ready for me to move in to until January, however Lola and Frank have asked me to join them at Featherwood Station for Christmas and I have accepted.'

'That works for me,' Francene said. 'We'll check out on Sunday and drive back in convoy then do the reverse trip next Thursday. Once settlement has taken place, I can camp in my little house while I sort out buying furniture and whatever else I need.'

'And will you stay with your friend again in Brisbane?' Eleanor's knowing gaze fixed on Francene and she grinned.

'Maybe.'

'Of course you will. I'm your friend and you will stay with me for the week while you tidy personal matters up and I attend to my appointments. Then we will return here to enjoy a wonderful wedding and festive season.'

They all laughed, and Briony pushed her chair back and picked up her empty glass. 'Right, ladies, let me grab the menu for you and then I'd better get back to the bar and let Alex return to the kitchen to cook whatever you select for your lunch.'

'Thanks, Briony,' Francene said.

'Yes, thank you so much,' Pam added.

Briony narrowed her eyes. 'Tomorrow night we've got quite a crowd coming here for dinner—it's usually our busiest night, but this time there will be a special reason to celebrate.' She smiled at the three women. 'I hope you'll all join us?'

'Apologies, Briony,' Pam said. 'I've made other arrangements.'

Francene looked at Eleanor, waited for her nod, then smiled. 'You can count on us, Briony.'

Briony winked at her and returned Francene's grin. 'Perfect! Any chance of you sparing a couple of hours tomorrow to help Alex with the preparation?'

Francene's heart soared. 'I'd love to.'

21

With Briony and Alex's wedding approaching rapidly, Ginny, Kirk, and Sophie languished over their breakfast, making plans for the following week.

'I'd like to bring the stud sheep in and sort them out for next Wednesday's sale,' Ginny said, wiping the sweat from her forehead. 'The bureau reckons we've got a heatwave coming next week, and it's best we don't stress them any more than necessary right before the sale. Goodness knows what they're calling this —winter?'

Kirk frowned, his eyes focused on Ginny. 'Are you alright, love? You look very hot but there's actually a nice, cool breeze today.'

Ginny pushed her chair back. 'I know. It's just this stupid body of mine,' she said crossly. 'It could be five degrees out there and I'm sure it would say we're having a tropical summer.'

Kirk and Sophie glanced at each other.

'Let's do it today. The yards around the woolshed are knee deep with grass, so we can select those to be sold and leave them there until Wednesday morning then take whichever ewes Ginny keeps back to a fresh paddock.'

'I can help,' Sophie said, raising her plastered wrist. 'I might not be able to drive or manhandle the girls for you, but I can still operate gates, chase them up the race—and write.'

Flapping a hand in front of her face, Ginny smiled wryly. 'Thanks, you two. This hot flush will be gone in a minute, and I'll be fine again.'

She collected the mugs and plates before slotting them into the dishwasher while Kirk and Sophie exchanged a grin.

'If you'd like to get the iPad and whatever else you need, Sophie, and I will take the ATV and bring the sheep in,' Kirk said.

'Now?' Ginny said.

'Sure. No time like the present.'

With the heat that burned through her body now fading, Ginny straightened, feeling more positive and energised. Although it would be hard parting with some bloodlines she'd taken years to perfect, it was all part of moving forward, responding to new demands to meet the market and being practical. As a wave of regret flowed through her, she steeled herself and followed Kirk and Sophie out the door.

AN HOUR LATER, Sophie followed the final sheep through the open gate and latched it behind her while Ginny watched and waited beside the shed.

It was only a small flock—less than one hundred not counting the seven remaining ewes she had introduced into the stud years earlier. They had been good mothers and despite vowing she'd never succumb to the golden rule of not getting attached to commercial animals, Ginny had. "They can live close to the sheds and keep the grass down for me," she'd declared when she'd decided to close the stud.

One by one, Ginny and Kirk inspected each animal while Sophie meticulously recorded ear tag numbers, weights, and ages. A small dot of marking paint was sprayed between the shoulders of each sheep, the colour denoting the distinctive groups so that when they reached the sale yards, they would be easily recognisable and drafted accordingly.

An hour on the phone with several smallholders who had purchased sheep from Ginny previously had been time well spent, and Ginny was confident she had made the right decision.

It was only as they herded the select few ageing ewes who would live out their lives on Featherwood Station up the lane toward the house paddock that Ginny allowed her stoicism to release. A deep, stabbing ache filled her chest. Not only was she experiencing the effects of aging herself—but saying goodbye to the small business that had carried her through the traumatic year following Lyndon's death left her feeling an emotional failure.

As though instinctively understanding, Kirk moved close to her and took her hand.

'New beginnings, eh?' he murmured.

She nodded silently, grateful that Sophie had opened gates.

'Yes. It's time to move on with new ideas and be thankful for all we have.'

22

The following evening, a steady stream of community members, those from farms around the area and visitors to the town, poured through the hotel doors.

Briony rushed into the kitchen where Alex was madly preparing large bowls of salad and a young girl introduced to Francene as Zoe—Lola and Frank's granddaughter—was elbow deep in soapy water, washing cooking utensils amongst a cloud of steam. Ann, Alex's regular assistant, was checking large trays of pork belly baking in the oven and Francene was putting the finishing touches to an enormous cake.

'Cripes! You should see the number of people in the bar already,' Briony said. 'Poor Sam and Mark are rushed off their feet, and Sophie's doing her best to do what she can with one hand to help them.'

Alex frowned. 'Is Sam okay? He's only been out of hospital one day so he might struggle a bit with the pressure.'

'Seems to be thriving on the attention he's getting at the moment. He was very popular before they went north and I think now that the whole town has heard about their accident, he and Sophie are receiving a hero's welcome. Anyway, we've got a new couple to town, Sheridan and Wayne, coming in at seven to take over the bar. They wanted a practice run so they can give a hand with our wedding next week if it's needed. So, this is perfect for them. By the time they arrive, most main courses will have been served and we can bring out the cake.'

'Great,' Alex chuckled. 'Lucky the fisho had an extra crate of barramundi this morning—I reckon we might need it.'

Francene placed the icing bag on the bench and flicked her tired hand at her side as she stepped back to scrutinise her work. The cake was three tiers high —the bottom layer a rich fruit cake, the centre a chocolate mud tier, and topping the extravagant creation was a light-as-air vanilla sponge cake. Creamy white icing covered the entire construction, and around each layer Francene had piped a row of colourful flowers interwoven with tiny green leaves and sprinkled with edible gold dust. Encircling the base, an assortment of farm animals and a bright green tractor made from fondant brought a smile to her face.

'What do you think?'

All four moved closer to her workstation, their incredulous expressions heightening Francene's satisfaction.

Alex spun the turntable slowly, his easy-going grin spreading wide. 'Unbelievable!'

'It's fabulous, Francene. You're so clever—and artistic,' Zoe said.

'Alex, look at the wee kelpie team ... Oh, and here's Akela!' Briony turned to face Francene. 'How did you know what the animals looked like? I didn't think you'd been to the farm yet?'

'I haven't, but Eleanor asked Lola if she had photos to help me and she did—dozens of them! I just hope I've got the detail right. I'll write their names on the top now and then it's finished.'

'Mum and Kirk will love it.'

'Do they know about tonight? I mean, that so many people are coming to celebrate their marriage?' Francene asked. She wasn't sure if this type of event was a regular thing in the country, but she knew that if she was to be the guest of honour with no warning, she would want to curl up under a table and hide.

'They've got no idea. Lola and Frank are waiting outside for them to arrive. I'm sure initially they'll just think we've got a bigger than usual crowd—which is something I'm proud to say has been happening over the past few months,' Briony said.

'The surprise won't last long,' Zoe said wryly. 'The second they enter the bar everyone will be hugging and congratulating them. I'm surprised that no one has blabbed already.'

Briony shrugged. 'Given they've been so busy with hay and everything else that's happened over the past couple of weeks, I doubt Mum has had a chance to talk to anyone outside the family.'

A cheer went up from multiple voices in the bar. 'Until now that is,' Briony added with a grin. 'Come on, let's get out there to welcome everyone.'

Overwhelmed with shyness, Francene skirted the packed room, finding Eleanor talking to a pretty, blonde-haired woman rocking a pram beside the door leading into the foyer.

'Gosh, there's standing room only tonight,' Eleanor said, bending forward to enable her voice to be heard amongst the excited chatter.

'I know. I didn't think there were this many people in Featherwood Falls.'

'It's not only the town. It's the entire district. Ginny is both well-respected and liked by many—and Kirk has won the hearts of all he meets. They make a great couple, and everyone wants to share in their excitement. And soon I'll be one of them. I've never felt so welcome anywhere in my whole life.'

An empathetic ache filled Francene. She under-stood exactly what Eleanor meant. All those years she had strived to be the person her parents wanted her to be, all those hours of study and homework trying to satisfy their wish for her to be like them—and her sister. Their goals had been to join the ranks of teaching in a highly esteemed private school before lecturing in universities all over the world, and they'd been flummoxed at Francene's lack of interest. Despite her family's encouragement and all her own efforts, her heart hadn't been in it and Francene had felt like a failure. But she wasn't the person they wanted her to be—or the person Kyle had wanted. She was a cook—a pastry chef and a good one. Reliving the delight that Briony and Alex had shown at her cake-decorating skills boosted her confidence. Now she was about to become a local resident herself—and she couldn't wait to prove to her family that her skills were every bit as important and satisfying as theirs had been.

Eleanor's voice penetrated her reflections. 'Francene, have you met Emma?' She turned toward the lady with the pram.

'Hello, Francene. I've heard so much about you,' Emma said, continuing to rock the pram gently. 'Please excuse my back—I'm trying to get this little one to sleep so we can enjoy our evening.'

Recognising the cherubic face of the baby lying peacefully, his rosebud mouth moving as though sucking an imaginary nipple, Francene smiled softly before lifting her gaze to meet Emma's. 'Hi, Emma. It's really nice to meet you—and to see your beautiful little boy again.'

An unfamiliar ache suddenly gripped her and for the first time in her life, she realised that motherhood, the tabu subject she had stored in the recesses of her mind for years, brought positive, even hopeful thoughts. Not that she hadn't wanted children—but how could she have coped with them—and Kyle. With his volatile mood swings and inability to manage finances, a family would have put an even bigger burden on her than she already had. But now he had gone, and life was changing. *Perhaps I should never say never.*

AN HOUR LATER, Francene squeezed into the chair beside Claire, casting a glance around the faces sitting at the long, narrow table that stretched almost the length of the dining room. Ginny and Kirk sat at one end while Lola and Frank sat at the other, with Emma and Ryan on either side of them and the pram containing the sleeping baby against the wall behind them. Along one side were Briony, Alex, Andrew, Sophie, and Sam, and on the other sat Eleanor, Rhys, Claire, and Francene. Between Francene and Ginny was a spare seat, and for a moment she wondered who was missing.

She didn't have to wait long as seconds later, the last person she'd expected—the man with the limp and kind smile she'd met at the shop—stood behind the vacant chair. She barely recognised him. His short brown hair and beard made him appear younger than she had first thought while the navy-coloured polo shirt he wore brought out the blue of his eyes. Even more noticeable was the fact that there was no sign of his walking stick. *What's his name again? Brian. No, that's not right. It's Bryn.*

'Hi again,' he said brightly as he lowered himself down carefully.

A warm flush rose up her neck and she lifted a hand to her cheek, willing the colour to fade—or better still, not to reach her face at all. 'Hi.' Words caught in her throat. How come he was here? Like her, was he a random invitee because that was the way they did things in this town? Or had someone decided having the two of them arrive in Feather-wood Falls on the same day was sufficient incentive to place them together, presuming they were already friends?

'Big crowd.'

'Yeah,' she squeaked, then cleared her throat. 'The whole town I reckon—and more.'

He chuckled—a friendly sound that made her turn

to face him. 'Like you, I've only been here a short time, but I can't believe how welcoming this town has been.'

She nodded. 'Me too.'

'Are you staying?'

'You mean—like living here?'

'Yes.'

'I am. I've just bought the cottage up the road. You?'

Her response appeared to have surprised him as his eyes widened.

'Same here—I mean—I haven't bought a house but am renting Claire and Rhys's place while I see how things go.'

'You're not from here then?'

'Nope.' He swivelled his head, appearing to study the crowd in the room. 'But I think I would like to hang around for a while.'

Before they could say more, a girl around Zoe's age appeared to take their orders while another three teenagers served adjacent tables.

Francene's appetite suddenly disappeared, the awareness of his proximity to her erasing all senses other than the heady confusion consuming her. A whiff of citrusy shampoo or aftershave drifted around her—a much more subtle and natural scent than the overpowering stuff Kyle had insisted on wearing.

Oh, for goodness' sake, get a grip on yourself. You need new friends and here's someone right next to you, possibly feeling every bit as overwhelmed as you.

'Noisy, isn't it?' he said, leaning toward her a little.

She nodded and smiled. 'Yeah. Maybe once everyone starts eating, it'll quieten down.'

Again, her awkwardness filled her with embarrassment, and she couldn't stop the colour from rising up her neck. *How am I going to cope with running a business if I can't even talk politely to this guy.*

She needn't have worried as the meals were served quickly, requiring only one or two visits to the kitchen by Alex, who, understandably, would want to ensure everyone received what they ordered.

Conversation with Bryn stalled as others took over, and it wasn't until Briony tapped her on the shoulder, whispering, 'Can you come and give us a hand with the cake?', that Francene pushed her chair back, excusing herself to Bryn.

'I'll be back in a minute. Just giving a hand with the next course.'

Not waiting for his response, she hurried after Briony—the barramundi, although delicious, weighing heavily in her stomach.

23

———

With Sam on one side and Alex on the other, the cake was carried to the centre of the dining room, where a small, cloth-covered table waited.

Everyone stood as Ginny and Kirk made their way to the cake, their admiration for its creator and decorator clear to all by their wide smiles.

Tears prickled behind Ginny's eyes as she cast a look around the crowd. They were family, her closest friends, and the community that had encompassed her through thick and thin over the past three decades and the Shepherd family for generations before her. Although she had recovered from the shock following their arrival, despite the surprise being a wonderful one, incredulity still filled her.

'So much for us wanting a quiet wedding with no fuss,' she whispered to Kirk.

'I know. But look at this cake! It's magnificent.'

The banging of a small hammer against an ancient copper saucepan found during the hotel renovations months earlier and kept for events such as this immediately quietened the crowd, and Briony and Claire stood on the opposite side of the cake from Ginny and Kirk.

'I'd like to thank you all for coming, especially with such short notice,' Briony said. 'Thanks also for purchasing dinner and helping us celebrate this special occasion—Mum and Kirk's marriage.'

'As you can see,' Claire intervened. 'We've got a pretty special dessert to share with you all—thanks to Lola for making the fruit layer and Alex for the chocolate and vanilla sponge layers. Not only have they baked this gorgeous creation, but our lovely new resident in Featherwood Falls, Francene, has decorated the entire thing for us.'

Everyone clapped, and Claire grabbed Francene by the arm, dragging her to her feet.

For a few seconds, Francene bowed her head as though too embarrassed to face the attention. But suddenly something must have struck a chord as she lifted her chin and a proud, wide smile spread across her face.

At that moment, the piano sounded from the

corner of the room and Ginny swung her gaze to where Emma sat with Zoe standing at her shoulder. The room fell silent as they sang the words of "All of Me" by John Legend. Refusing to allow the tears to fall, Ginny dabbed a scrunched tissue against her face. Kirk wrapped his arm around her waist as the crowd swayed with the music before clapping and whistling as the song ended.

Numerous members of the community stepped forward, edging for a position to admire and photograph Francene's work while whispers spread about the new lady in town.

Then Briony placed a beautiful antique silver knife in Ginny's hand. More photos were taken, and together, Kirk and Ginny cut the first slice of the top layer. Cheers went up as a queue formed, and with Ginny's help, Briony and Alex began slicing and serving the celebration cake.

Through it all, baby Liam never stirred.

LATER THAT NIGHT, Francene lay on her bed in the room above the bar, the last calls of goodbye and the slamming of car doors echoing in her ears.

What on earth made me do that?

While accepting Bryn's invitation to join him for coffee the following morning in Lola's store wasn't exactly a "hot" date, her response had shocked her. It had been difficult to have a conversation with the amount of chatter in the dining room, and after the cake had been consumed and most families with children had headed home, Sam had turned up the sound system in the bar and those remaining had either sung along or danced—or both. In a whirlwind, Claire had introduced her to so many people, Francene's head had spun. She couldn't remember most names, but there had been a few familiar faces she had seen on her morning walks and around town. A couple that had caught her eye as they danced, cheek to cheek and taking turns swinging a young boy of about six or seven around them, had stopped to speak to her again. She had been grateful for them repeating their names —Ashleigh, Damian, and the boy was Charlie. She remembered Ashleigh's cheery morning hello as she hurried through the school gate on the day Francene was later than usual returning to the hotel from her walk. Charlie had been with the auburn-haired woman, and she had presumed they were mother and son, despite the difference in looks. A five-minute chat with Ashleigh before the music got too loud to hear properly confirmed she was one of the teachers, Charlie was Damian's son, and that she and Damian were getting married nearby at a place called "Kallala" on New Year's Eve.

Lying on her back, Francene smiled softly.

Ashleigh had been only one of the fresh faces she had felt an immediate bond with. Another was Sophie, the delightful Scottish girl who'd been injured in the accident two days before she'd arrived in town. Like her brother Alex, Sophie had an easy-going friendliness about her and a delightful sense of humour. The way she'd described their accident far more light-heartedly than Francene was sure she would have felt at the time and her strong accent and descriptions had brought a laugh from all those sitting in the bar. The big New Zealand man introduced as Sam had held Sophie's hand at every opportunity and his caring gaze toward her left no doubt they were a couple in love.

Bryn had stayed until after Ginny and Kirk left for home but had said little. So the coffee invitation had come as even more of a surprise to Francene, and the response that burst from her had been totally unexpected—at least to her own ears.

Beaming, Bryn had given her a small nod, smiling as he left the room, his limp barely noticeable.

Despite attempting to convince herself she did not want another relationship—she had a business to build and needed to remain professional and friendly toward everyone in the town—a small voice niggled inside her head. One that reminded her she was an attractive, thirty-five-year-old woman—and she wasn't dead yet.

TUCKED into a corner on the side veranda of Lola's store, Francene's eyes met Bryn's across the table.

'Shall I pour?' She grinned, breaking the awkward silence.

'Thanks.' He returned her smile and chuckled. 'This reminds me of having tea with my grandmother yonks ago.'

'Oh! Am I that old-fashioned?' Francene's retort was quick and a little sharper than she intended.

He shook his head, his eyes wide with mortification. 'Sorry. I didn't mean it like that. I-I just ...' He trailed off with a shrug. 'My grandmother and I were close and shared our love of tea—so sitting here kind of brought those memories back.'

Francene smiled again. 'I understand and I'm sorry too. I didn't mean it as a criticism.' She leaned back in her chair, holding the thick ceramic cup in both hands. 'I am old-fashioned in many ways. I love old furniture, fine china, and good manners. And I've just contradicted myself in that regard.'

'So, we're even. Shall we start again?' He took a swallow of his tea and replaced the cup in the saucer. 'Tell me more about your interests—this old furniture that you like, to begin with.'

Hesitantly, she began describing the dressing table that had once belonged to her father's grandmother, a pretty writing desk that had come from France with her mother decades earlier, and a commode cabinet she had picked up from a garage sale. 'Not sure what I'll use it for, but it makes a nice bedside table,' she laughed. 'What about you?'

As their conversation morphed from furniture to hobbies and past workplaces, Francene relaxed, surprised to discover how easy Bryn was to talk with. There was no hint of dominance or one-upmanship, no boasting about sporting prowess, and definitely no mention of past relationships.

The generous-sized teapot emptied quickly, and the lamingtons were enjoyed with coconut-finger-licking delight as the hour passed in a flash.

It was Bryn who moved first. 'It's been a lovely morning. Thank you, Francene.' He screwed his face into an apologetic frown. 'I'm sorry I can't stay. I'm making something for my parents and if I don't get back to it, it won't be ready for Christmas.'

She shot to her feet, knocking the table with her leg and grabbing the tiny milk jug before it toppled over. 'Oh, sorry.' Heat flared on her cheeks.

'It's all good,' he said. 'Perhaps we can do this again soon—especially as we're both about to become locals.'

A rush of warmth flooded her as they stood and strolled through the shop before halting beside his car.

'I doubt we'll be considered locals—I think that takes about five generations.'

He laughed then, a deep-throated, full-bodied laugh that made crinkles around his eyes and showed strong, white teeth.

Clasping her hands between his, he leaned forward and for a moment she thought he was about to kiss her. Uncertain if she was relieved or disappointed when he didn't, she almost missed his last words. 'You're right. But this feels like a pleasant town to hang around in, and you never know, perhaps we'll both find our happy place.'

His touch burned through her skin as, seemingly reluctant to do so, he released her hands and opened the car door. 'See you again soon?'

She nodded. 'Sounds good.'

Then she lifted her hand in a tiny wave as he drove away, her heart thumping inside her chest.

Confusion wrestled with delight as she walked along the footpath. 'I've told you before,' she muttered to herself. 'Men are nothing but trouble, so what on earth are you doing?' But as she voiced the words, a new hope blossomed inside her, erasing some of her doubts. There were kind, genuine people in this world. Eleanor was proof of that. And maybe, just maybe, Bryn might be another.

24

Ginny woke slowly, squinting at the morning sun shining through the open French doors. Kirk's long legs spread over the sheet that had been thrown back in the heat of the night. Unusually high temperatures had kept them both tossing and turning, despite the more-than-usual drinks they had consumed the previous night, and Ginny felt as though she hadn't slept at all.

Grateful for Sophie and Sam choosing to stay at the hotel where they could help Briony and Alex clean up after the big night, Ginny stretched, her weary body luxuriating in their peace and lack of responsibilities. Well, human ones anyway, she thought as her mind filled with farm chores that needed to be done more regularly in hot weather. Checking water troughs was a daily job and keeping a close eye on the rapidly drying grass and surrounding bushland was essential, not only for the animal's welfare but also for bush-fire prevention.

Kirk's arm reached over her, snuggling her perspiring body against his.

'You're hot.'

She snorted. 'Not sure how I should take that, but it's going to be another scorcher—and this body of mine is already unhappy.' Sitting up, she glanced at the clock then kissed him and slid out of bed. 'It's eight-thirty already. Poor animals will think we've forgotten about them. I'm hopping in the shower.'

'Righto. I'm guessing that's my cue to get up?'

She laughed and ambled across the hall to the bathroom, stripping off her nightie as she went. 'You got it—unless you feel like joining me?'

'You know what?' A thump sounded from his side of the bed as he spoke. 'I reckon we throw a flask of coffee and those croissants you bought yesterday into a backpack and head to the falls. A refreshing dip is just what we need to get the day started.'

About to turn on the tap in the shower, Ginny paused. A swim did sound enticing—and with only the two of them there, they could sprawl out on the rocks afterwards to dry off and eat breakfast.

'Sounds like a lovely way to start the day. You put the coffee on, and I'll get dressed.'

After releasing the kelpies from their kennels, they

made their way along the track toward the bush in the distance. Once over the ridge that separated the creek from the house, the sound of water reached them—and ten minutes later they stood in the shade of the grotto, shed their clothing, and plunged into the pool hand in hand.

'Yikes! It's freezing!' Ginny shrieked. She stroked across to the opposite side before returning to the dogs.

'Come on, girls and boys. Jump in.'

Kirk laughed and did as she asked, dragging himself out and leaping again, sending a wave of soaking cold water over both Ginny and the dogs. Three kelpies leapt in, slowly followed by a fourth and then a fifth. But no matter how much they called, Drum refused to join them.

'Poor little guy. He's never forgotten what happened that day Lyndon died,' Ginny said quietly. She dragged herself onto the rocks and gathered him in her arms. 'Come on, mate. Just a quick swim to keep me company,' she coaxed.

If he could have given a reluctant shrug, Ginny was certain he would have. But instead, he scrabbled against her, his front legs wrapped around her neck as she turned on her back and floated toward Kirk.

With the swim lasting less than a minute, Ginny sat wrapped in a towel with Drum at her side while Kirk poured their coffee and the other dogs continued to paddle about in the pond.

'This has to be the best thing we ever did on this farm,' Ginny said, quietly studying the pool enveloped by its assortment of rocks. 'In weather like this, it's pretty hard to beat.'

She met Kirk's kind, considerate eyes. They rarely discussed their past relationships—her marriage to Lyndon and his to Katie. They didn't need to. Each of them had lost a partner they loved, and their mutual understanding was part of the bond that had brought them together, allowing them both a second chance at love.

'It's perfect.' He passed her a mug of coffee and a croissant filled with ham and cheese. 'I appreciate the work you both did, especially your efforts to restore the entire property to the way it was—replanting trees and repairing waterways to what they should be.' He pointed to the kangaroo scat nearby. 'Even this pool, although man-made, is a glorious spot for wildlife to drink and rest.'

'True. Speaking of which—I guess we'd better get dressed and do the rounds.'

Kirk brushed the flakes of pastry from his hands and finished his coffee. Then he pulled Ginny to her feet and hugged her tightly against him. 'Coming here was one of the best decisions I've ever made.'

She smiled up at him. 'Yeah. And letting you come

and stay, especially when half the town were thinking you might be Lyndon's murderer, was one of the best decisions I've ever made.'

They laughed again as Ginny glanced up at the sky, her smile fading quickly. 'If the weather stays like this all week, it won't only be the stock who'll be lethargic—Alex's poor parents will cook.'

'Is it Monday they arrive?'

'Yes. Sophie and Alex will pick them up from the airport and Briony and Sam will stay here to run the pub.' She chuckled. 'Apparently, Briony and Alex have arranged for the four of them to have a few days away together after the wedding—to show them a little of our country before the roads and accommodation fill up with Christmas holiday-makers.'

'Sounds like an interesting honeymoon.' Kirk laughed.

'That's what I mean. Still, I agree with Briony—they've been living together for years now, and Aileen and Bruce are only in Australia for a few weeks. They need to make the most of their time here and after they've gone back to Scotland and life returns to normal here, Mark and Ann have said they'd take care of the hotel while Briony and Alex have a break on their own.'

'Sounds good. What about us? When are we going to have a break on our own?' Kirk asked.

For a moment they stared at each other, Ginny struggling to read Kirk's expression.

Then his solemn face softened, and he grinned. 'You know the jar of mining finds I've been hoarding away over the past couple of years?'

'Yes,' she said slowly, uncertain where his thoughts were taking them.

'I rang the agent in Brisbane the other day. It seems gold is at an all-time high at the moment, so I'm going to cash in what I've got.'

'Good on you. You deserve a good price after all your hard work extracting it. What are your plans for the money—a new car?'

They both roared with laughter. Kirk's battered old LandCruiser had done so many kilometres Ginny was astounded it was still functioning. But it was—and with Kirk's mechanical expertise and care of the vehicle, the odometer would no doubt do another hundred thousand kilometres before he would consider replacing it.

His expression became solemn as he placed a hand on each of her shoulders and their eyes met. 'I know how worried you are about Nigel returning to live next door—so I thought we might make an offer to buy him out. What do you think?'

'What?' Wide eyed, her forehead creased. 'How can we possibly afford to do that? We've just cleared the mortgage on this place and with the price of sheep and cattle, I doubt we'd be able to raise enough to get another loan, even with Mum's inheritance and the proceeds of your hard-earned gold.' His shoulders sagged, and she regretted her outburst.

'Yeah, I know. It was just a thought.'

Her heart melted. Although they were both in their fifties and the argument she had put forward about borrowing money—and the subsequent stress that would be likely to cause them both—was sound, it was the thought that counted. His willingness to do something so generous in order to save her from worrying brought tears to her eyes.

'No, we can't do that. It's a vegetable farm and we're both already busy enough with this place.'

He hugged her to him once more before stepping back and meeting her eyes again. 'You're right.' Then a cheeky grin spread across his face. 'I have another suggestion—one that we can afford and would put the proceeds from my mining adventures to a good use.'

Intrigue pushed the thought of purchasing Glenrowan from her mind. 'What?'

'A holiday. I thought we might have a trip somewhere.'

Ginny's eyebrows rose. 'Really! Where to?'

'Canada. Alaska. Scotland. I don't mind, but it's time we had a proper holiday—and I'd kinda like to see a bit of the world.'

For a beat she felt nothing as she processed this

suggestion. She had considered adding another farm-stay cottage to the property with her inheritance. But even that would increase her workload—and she wasn't sure she wanted more guests than what she already catered for. Kirk's suggestion brought an entire world to her, one that although it had flittered through her mind, she had never seriously considered—the farm came first. Excitement blossomed then swelled inside her. An overseas trip with Kirk! Goosebumps formed on her arms. It was so totally unexpected and out of left field.

What a fabulous idea!

'Oh! Oh!' was all she could say, but her smile said it all.

She threw her arms around his neck as all thoughts of Nigel's parole, the heat, Briony's wedding, and the waiting animals faded into oblivion.

25

———————

*A*lthough tired after the drive to Brisbane, Francene and Eleanor sat up late discussing plans for the next few days, their voices rising in pitch as excitement built.

'I'll organise a removalist first thing in the morning, then go to the storage place and collect the boxes my baking equipment is in,' Francene said. 'Then, while you're attending your appointments, I'll buy the ingredients I'll need and—if you're sure you don't mind—will have a practice run through of some of the petit fours and pastries I used to make. We can have a tasting session and decide which ones I should make for the wedding.'

Eleanor rubbed her thin, veined hands together. 'Ooh, that sounds wonderful. I don't bake much these days, but I'm a good taste-tester.' Laughing, they each continued with their lists. 'I'm a firm believer in being organised. That way neither of us will forget anything and we can get back to Featherwood Falls as soon as possible.'

Francene smiled in agreement, the butterflies in her stomach leaping around wildly as enthusiasm grew. 'I still can't believe it.'

'I know, dear. It's been one of those weeks, hasn't it?'

'It has—and I'm so grateful to you for inviting me to stay.'

Eleanor flapped her hand in dismissal. 'Pfft. I enjoy your company and can't see why our companionship can't continue for another few days. Now that my house is only weeks away, I suppose I should think about packing up a few things here—and discussing the sale of this place with an agent.' A thread of anxiety accompanied her words.

The bewildered look on her friend's face sent a surge of empathy through Francene. 'I can help. We'll collect some boxes tomorrow if you like—then while I'm here, we can go through one room at a time and you can decide what you want to take to your new house and what you want to give to charity—or some-where else.'

Eleanor's face lightened a little as she rose to her feet. 'Thank you, dear. Now it's bedtime for me I think.'

'Me too.'

Half an hour later, Francene lay on the narrow bed in Eleanor's spare bedroom, her head spinning. Less than two weeks earlier, she had been camped in her tiny tent, homeless and struggling with what to do next. *Now I have a generous and caring new friend and am about to own a home—and start a business.* As the thoughts ran riot, she recalled the welcoming, almost excited delight that Alex, Briony, Lola, and Frank had exuded when she had discussed her prospective new venture with them. There had been no hesitation or hint of resentment from any of them. She rolled over and picked up the pen and list from the bedside table.

Using the semi-light filtering through the window from the streetlight outside, she added, "Buy flowers for Lola and Frank and Briony and Alex on the way back to Featherwood Falls", and "Talk to the council about requirements to operate a café". Then she rolled on her side facing a large bookcase and breathed deeply, allowing the scent of lavender and old books to fill her senses.

THE FOLLOWING days flew as both Francene and Eleanor arranged for the removal company to transfer Francene's belongings to Featherwood Falls the following week—the last delivery before the Christmas break, while Eleanor settled on the last week of January.

Eleanor began sorting through accumulated books, clothing, and items she had forgotten she owned while Francene refreshed her ideas in the kitchen, relieved the skills she had learned a decade earlier had not been forgotten. Instead, new inspiration fuelled her enthusiasm, and by late on Wednesday, she had concocted a range of tiny pastries and cakes for Alex and Briony to sample. Once they had made their choice, Francene would spend Friday baking, including icing the wedding cake. Final touches for both the petit fours and cake would be completed on Saturday morning.

Although this would be cutting things fine with the marriage service taking place at three-thirty on Saturday afternoon, Francene was confident everything would be as Briony and Alex wished—and she crossed her fingers that what she presented would help boost the beginnings of her own new business.

After breezily informing her the council office would close for the Christmas period, the planning officer advised it was unlikely she would hear from them before mid-January, even if she emailed the required documents to them that day. But Francene would not let herself become despondent. *I'm over that stage of my life. I will not look back,* she reiterated with silent determination. Pouring through the documents relating to the physical requirements of the building before a licence to operate a food business could be granted, she submitted the completed documents and set a mental date to open on the first week of February. With the residue of her savings, she would employ someone to update the kitchen and install the required toilet facilities to meet council requirements as soon as Christmas was over—and then, reassured by Eleanor that it would be a roaring success, she would begin her new life.

For the first time in a long time, she was free to make the decisions without influence or ridicule from Kyle, her sister, or anyone else. But as she rattled her plans off breathlessly to Eleanor, she couldn't help but notice the fleeting frown of doubt that touched the older woman's face.

Her stomach clenched. From nowhere, a vision of Bryn flashed through her mind. Despite his physical challenges, he had not given up. He'd survived whatever had happened and, although she didn't know the details, she had a gut feeling he was taking a similar path to her own and forging ahead down a new road of life.

She grinned at Eleanor. 'I might be a little optimistic about my dates, but even if it takes longer, it *will* happen.'

Eleanor returned the smile and nodded. 'Of course it will. And we have each other to share problems with now.'

Without thinking, Francene did something she had not done in years. She gave the woman a hug.

26

As he strolled around Stanthorpe, ideas swirled in Bryn's head. Although primarily a rural town, there was a creative vibe—evident by the eclectic mix of artwork, crafts, and vibrant colours in shop fronts, gardens, and even in the streets. He liked it and especially liked the fact that no one seemed to have even noticed his limp or walking stick. As he wandered, people smiled at him and said hello, looking him directly in the eye. It was something he was getting used to in Featherwood Falls but had never experienced in the city. Here, the people seemed unafraid of being themselves. Dressed in classic country clothing or brightly coloured patchwork pants or skirts that swished along the pavement, even their assortment of headgear kept the smile on his face—an

Akubra, a peaked cap, purple hair, and a mix of floppy-brimmed hats, all helped his sense of comfort.

After purchasing a supply of groceries, he visited the hardware stores and finally the timber yards. Pleased with his new chainsaw and myriad of other tools and equipment, he fuelled his ute and headed back to Featherwood Falls.

For the next few days, except for his increasingly more strenuous regime of strengthening exercises and his daily walk to the falls on Ginny's farm, which she had kindly allowed him to continue with, he spent his time in the shed, sawing, trimming, sanding, and hand-carving. Every now and then, he looked out into the sunshine and wished he had that someone special in his life. *Perhaps I should rescue a dog from the pound?*

By Friday, his first project was complete, and he stood back to admire it. The protective coating of oil wasn't quite dry, but a warm glow of satisfaction and pride filled his chest.

He retreated to the house and boiled the kettle, spooned a generous dollop of herbal tea into the ceramic teapot he'd picked up at the second-hand shop for two dollars, and waited for it to steep. Wandering onto the front veranda, he glanced at the rickety chair beside the door. Well used and desperate for mainte-nance, a vision of his next project flashed through his mind—something more suitable. What the porch needed was a longer, curved-seated bench with a comfortable back to lean on and wide armrests to place his cup of tea on. Not one of those cheap, flimsy-timbered versions sold by large hardware conglomerates, but something he could stretch out on—perhaps even lie on at night when he couldn't sleep and needed to breathe in the night sky and watch the shooting stars.

After finishing two full mugs of tea, he returned to the shed and took photos of his creation from every angle.

Then, listening to the twinges of well-rehearsed pain in his back and hip, he conceded, picked up his keys, and headed to his ute.

Neatly tucked between the general store and the post office, the rainbow-coloured shed glowed in the sunlight. On his previous jaunt into the village to collect fresh milk and a magazine to read, Bryn had stopped to talk to Frank, who was fitting a Perspex window to the front façade. The building reminded him of the cubbyhouse his grandfather had built for him and Mae when they were young. The older boys had scoffed, assuring them they were far too old for playing stupid kids' games, but he and Mae had loved it and spent many hours curled up on cushions reading—often when their father was in one of his bad moods and they needed a place to hide.

Instead of heading straight into the shop, he paused outside the little building, smiling at the sign on the door—"Come and Find Me". He opened the latch—an old-fashioned lever that nestled into a U-shaped socket—and peered inside. Both sides were lined with shelves, some already full of books of every genre and condition. At the back, a narrow bench and a pile of cushions squeezed between the bookshelves, giving just enough space for a child to sit and thumb through the stack of children's books contained on the bottom shelf of each side.

His heart leapt with delight as he stood, mesmerised.

'What do you reckon?'

He jumped at the sound of Lola's cheery voice.

'Sorry, love. Didn't mean to startle you.' She held a pile of books in her arms and angled her head toward the shelves. 'Got a few more to offload.' Chuckling, she added, 'We've had that many books dropped off to kickstart the exchange project, I reckon Frank will have to build a bigger one somewhere else shortly.'

'I think it's a great idea,' Bryn said. 'I actually popped down to pick up a magazine or something new to read—but this looks like an even better option.'

'Well. That's what it's for. Here.' She thrust the books she carried toward him. 'Start with these and perhaps you wouldn't mind putting anything that doesn't appeal to you on the shelves?'

'Sure. Thanks.'

She stepped back, allowing the afternoon sun to shine through the gap and onto the shelves where seconds earlier, her stocky figure had shaded. 'Frank and me are about to have a cuppa. When you've chosen your books, why don't you join us? We haven't seen you all week.'

He grinned at her friendly invitation. Would he ever get used to this casual and sociable banter? 'Thanks. I'll be in shortly.'

Ten minutes later, he plonked the four books he had chosen on the passenger seat of the ute and entered the store.

Frank and Lola were sitting at the same table on the side veranda where, almost three weeks earlier, he had been when Lola had cleaned and dressed his hand. It seemed like forever ago. Beside them, a pram containing a chubby baby making an assortment of noises thrashed a toy around with an unsteady arm, crashing it against the side of the pram and chortling. Lola and Frank's daughter-in-law was also seated at the table.

He couldn't remember her name and for a moment, he paused.

'Come on over here, Bryn,' Lola called. 'Emma's joining us, and Ryan is making the coffee.'

As if on cue, the hissing of the coffee machine sounded behind him, and he took a seat next to Frank.

Moments passed as the coffees and lamingtons were shared, Ryan took a seat, and Emma introduced baby Liam to him. It took Bryn a few minutes to realise that the familiar awkwardness he had felt in similar situations since his accident was no longer present. The conversation was warm, the welcome genuine. He blinked. Had his two years of pain and recovery damaged his trust that much? He'd never been outgoing, but during the assortment of occupations he'd had in over twenty years, he'd always worked diligently, got along with his peers, and joined in on every social occasion going. In the early days, girlfriends had been a given, even if they hadn't lasted long. But from the day of his accident—which just happened to occur during a girlfriend drought—shock, pity, and obvious discomfort had shown in the eyes of his friends and workmates. One by one, their visits had decreased until he was left with just Mae, his caring, beautiful, and bossy little sister.

Lost in his reflections, he missed Lola's question and squirmed as he felt everyone's eyes on him.

'Sorry.'

'I asked what you've been doing lately. Are you enjoying being in your own place? Well, not that it is your own, but I guess it is for a while.' She laughed, and Bryn smiled in response.

'Had a look around Stanthorpe. Bought some bits and pieces—and I've been doing a bit of woodwork.'

Frank leaned closer, turning an ear toward him that Bryn suddenly realised contained a hearing aid. 'Woodwork, you say?'

'Yeah. I quite like making things. Worked for a cabinet-maker in the UK for a while a decade or so back. He taught me a lot and I wouldn't have left except that he had a heart attack and sold his business. Without me attached.'

'Oh.' Frank sat back and their eyes met. 'What have you been making?'

Bryn pulled his phone out of his pocket. 'Probably easier if I show you.' He tapped in his code and brought up the photos. Then, expanding them to fill the screen, he passed the phone around.

'Wow!' Lola took it first while Frank fumbled for his glasses and Emma waited patiently. Lola's eyes widened as her gaze alternated between Bryn's and the screen several times. 'How did you do the carving?'

Frank reached for the phone as Bryn shrugged.

'I made the back as one piece—traced the design onto the wood first, then lay it on the workbench and worked on it in much the same way a seamstress would work on a patchwork quilt, I guess. Once I was happy with the carved section, I shaped the rest to fit the backs of two adults, side by side in comfort, then I made the rest of the seat, carved the legs using a lathe, and put it all together.'

Meeting the amazed admiration from his audience sent a hot thrill through him. *They love it!*

'Would you make us one, Bryn?' Emma asked. 'It would be perfect on our veranda.'

'And us too?' Lola looked at Frank. 'Or perhaps two single seats. They would be perfect in front of the book exchange. If they weren't too big or heavy, Frank could put them out each morning and lock them inside the wee building at night.'

As the conversation continued around him, so too did the burning delight inside him. He couldn't wait to get back to the shed and design his next project.

Later, he pulled the door toward him while giving the family a small wave, almost crashing into Francene.

'Oh, sorry,' she said.

'My fault. Wasn't looking.'

For a few seconds, they stood in mutual silence, neither moving.

'Hello, Francene. Forgotten something, love?' Lola broke the spell, and Francene stepped around Bryn, apologising again.

'Butter. We've run out of butter, and I've almost finished.'

Bryn's eyebrows rose, a reluctance to leave pinning him firmly to the spot. *I wonder what she's making.*

'How does the cake look? Is Briony happy with it?' Lola continued.

'Oh yes. They're both thrilled—and they love the petit fours.' The joy in Francene's voice was palpable and, for a reason he couldn't comprehend, his body bloomed with empathy and happiness for her.

It took him a moment, but then he remembered. Tomorrow was to be Briony and Alex's wedding. The event that, while not exactly stopping the nation, would be the occasion of the year for the Featherwood Falls population. According to snippets of overheard discussion while he had been at Ginny's, only a group of around eighty family and friends would attend the reception in the hotel, but most of the town would turn out to watch the first wedding to be held in the little church in a decade. He wasn't sure if Francene was to be a guest, but he hoped everyone enjoyed their day and it sounded as though Francene's contribution to the food had already been tested, approved, and appreciated.

He also hoped his woodwork would bring the same positive reaction from his parents as it had from the Brown family.

Ginny slid out of bed as dawn sent a pink glow into their bedroom. Her stomach dropped, reflecting on the wise old saying "Red sky at night, shepherd's delight. Red sky in the morning, shepherd's warning". She hoped it would not be the case today of all days. While rain was almost always welcome, today was one of those exceptions where she wished for good weather—not too hot or windy and preferably no rain. She let out a big sigh.

'Don't tell me,' Kirk grumbled.

'Okay. I won't. If it's going to rain, we'll just have to hope it holds off until tomorrow—or at least until after the service and photos.'

'Fair enough. My priority is to get that bottom lucerne paddock baled.' He stretched, stepped out of bed, and wandered to the glass doors that led onto the veranda. Frowning, he turned to Ginny, who was dressing with anxious, staccato movements. 'The light's kind of eerie.'

She nodded. 'Yep. Come on. No time to waste today. While you get on the tractor and bale that hay, I'll cut the greenery and flowers we need and deliver them to the church. Mary Passmore and Jean Hillier said they'd be there at seven to decorate.'

Kirk obediently headed to the bathroom, and within fifteen minutes, Ginny had the coffee brewed, toast and eggs ready to serve, and was feeding the cats.

Working quickly, she did the outdoor animal-feeding rounds, then returned to the laundry where she gathered her gloves, secateurs, and foliage baskets. As some of the wedding photos were to be taken in and around the homestead, Ginny had put an extra effort into the summer gardens. The roses had never bloomed so well, liberally dosed with fertiliser at regular intervals together with the multiple punnets of seedlings she had sown in spring that now spread in a carpet of colour amongst the swathes of green lawn. The liberal watering required to achieve the garden splendour had left the house tanks almost empty. So, while she hoped for Briony's sake it didn't rain, several days of steady downpours were exactly what the district needed.

By quarter to seven, Ginny was on her way to the church with baskets of flowers lined up along the back seat, the car boot full of greenery, and three buckets of long-stemmed roses jammed together on the front passenger-side footwell.

At nine o'clock, she returned to the farm, leaving Mary and Jean with their additional helpers, who had turned up at a more respectable hour to help finish decorating the church.

The rhythmic chug of the hay baler soothed her frazzled nerves as she boiled the kettle and filled a flask with tea for Kirk. Any threat of rain approaching when a crop was waiting to be harvested was nail-biting, but where machinery was involved, the anxiety seemed to escalate—the dread of that sudden silence that signalled a breakdown of some sort.

Fortunately, today the gods were with them, and Kirk inched the baler down the final windrow just as the clouds parted and the sun swept over the paddocks, drying any remnants of morning dew.

Wordlessly, Kirk beamed at Ginny as she handed him the flask, and they both huffed a relieved breath.

'Now to get it into the shed.' She glanced around, her hopes torn. It was a good crop. Every bale was close to its partner, meaning that while they would have more than they expected, it also meant it would take more time than they could spare to load it onto the truck and stack it in the shed.

Her thoughts dashed from one possibility to another. No point in asking Claire to help. She and

Sophie were Briony's bridesmaids and would already be in the process of having their hair and makeup done in addition to keeping Briony out of the kitchen and concentrating on herself. Andrew would be in the same predicament as her and Kirk. Glenrowan's hay had been cut the same day as theirs and most of their staff had finished harvesting tomatoes and been given two weeks off for Christmas.

She ran through a mental list of friends she might have called on, but everyone had a reason for unavailability next to their name. Mostly because they were also coming to the wedding and had their own businesses to organise beforehand. No point wasting time thinking about it. *Just get on with it.*

After striding to the truck, she waited for Kirk to climb in with her before driving to the shed on the far side of the paddock. Kirk slid the heavy doors aside and they dragged out the hay-loader, fixed it to the driver's side of the truck tray, then, while Kirk returned the tractor and baler to the machinery shed near the house, Ginny began driving the truck around seemingly endless circles, checking as each bale reached the top of the loader and spilled into a heap on the tray. After every few bales, she stopped, climbed onto the back of the truck, and stacked the bales in a neat pattern, allowing room for the next load before returning to the driver's seat and continuing.

With Kirk's arrival, the pace quickened. While

Ginny drove the truck and loader, Kirk balanced on the tray, rhythmically grasping the bale with muscle-bound arms as each square of compressed lucerne rose to the top. Then, after swinging it into position in the stack, he repeated the procedure. As soon as the truck was full, Ginny reversed it into the shed where she and Kirk transferred the bales onto the ever-increasing stash of hay that was already halfway to the roof.

By noon, both were exhausted and there were still a hundred bales left in the paddock waiting for their turn to be picked up and tucked into the shed.

'No more!' Ginny called to Kirk. 'We've got one hour to have lunch and get showered and dressed for the wedding.' Running a dirty hand through her wild, brown locks, tears welled. 'And I have no idea what I'm going to do with my hair.'

Frank would deliver the girls to the homestead for photos to be taken between one and one-thirty that afternoon. After much discussion about where the wedding party's preparation should take place, it had been decided that the hotel would remain the venue for the hairdresser and makeup artist to attend to the women, then Lola would assist them to dress. As the "official" dressmaker, she had taken great pride in ensuring Briony, Claire, and Sophie's gowns were stitch-perfect, and because of her attention to detail, Briony had happily agreed Lola was the right person—able to tweak anything if required. Meanwhile, Alex and Sam had joined Rhys at the police-station quarters to prepare for the event under the supervision of Alex's parents.

'Righto, love. You head to the house, and I'll lock up here. See you in a few minutes.'

Ginny clamped her lips together and nodded, determined to control her emotions. With physical exhaustion and the pressure to get everything right for her daughter's special day, Ginny knew better than anyone that once the tears began falling, she would be helpless to stop them.

THE SUN CONTINUED to shine despite the increasing humidity, and Ginny wasn't sure how everything had fallen into place as easily as it had. But with Claire twisting Ginny's freshly washed hair into an elegant pleat at the base of her neck, Sophie one-handedly pouring a glass of nerve-settling wine for everyone and Kirk sharing repeated admiring comments, the five of them appeared calm and serene by the time the photographer, Keely, arrived.

After cheerily announcing the guys were ready and that Aileen was keeping a tight rein on the amount of alcohol consumed, Keely confirmed the photos she had taken of Alex, his parents, and attendants would be everything Briony hoped for. Then she efficiently began arranging the girls and going about her business without fuss.

On the dot of three-fifteen, two washed and polished Isuzu dual-cabs arrived at the farm—one driven by Alex's friend Damian, and the other by Quinn, the school principal, who had been delegated by Alex to find suitable vehicles for the occasion.

Ginny, Claire, and Sophie got carefully into Damian's while Keely assisted Briony into Quinn's. Kirk slid in beside Briony and the procession moved along the driveway.

From the front passenger seat in the first vehicle, Ginny glanced in the outside mirror, releasing a slow breath.

The wedding had finally arrived and, although appreciative of the help everyone had given Briony and Alex, an ominous flutter stirred deep inside Ginny's belly. She would be relieved when the day was behind them.

28

___

hat was I worrying about? Ginny thought as she turned to face the proud smile on both Kirk's and Briony's faces as they walked up the aisle. Her frantic, hair-tearing morning drifted into oblivion as the word-perfect ceremony proceeded, and in seemingly no time, the huge crowd that swarmed the back of the church and spilled outside beamed with joy and sprinkled both Briony and Alex with rose petals as they stepped into what was becoming a steamy afternoon.

Aileen squeezed Ginny's arm as they ambled slowly down the aisle. 'Did you ever think we would actually reach this day?' she said in her soft Scottish accent.

Ginny smiled at her. An older replica of her daughter, Sophie, Aileen had seemed like a long-lost friend —a result of the many FaceTime calls exchanged between Australia and Scotland over the past year or more. Bruce, too, felt like a brother to Ginny with his calm, cheerful demeanour and wide smile so similar to that of Alex. Despite both Alex and Sophie sharing their mother's colouring, there was a strong family likeness between father and son. From the moment they had stepped out of the car on arrival at the hotel, Ginny had experienced a sense of relief. It was as though her non-existent extended family had arrived to support her.

More photography continued outside the church before the cavalcade of cars returned to Featherwood Station for pictures to be taken of the wedding party and families in Ginny's colour-filled garden.

By the time they all arrived at the hotel, trays of Francene's tiny canapes were being passed around by teenagers smartly dressed in white shirts and black pants, while Mark and his assistants were plying the crowd with trays filled with glasses of wine, soft drink, and beer.

To Ginny, the evening seemed to disappear in a whirlwind as dinner was announced, followed by speeches, and the cutting of the magnificent cake, decorated with a circle of fondant Scotch thistles in green and lavender-blue rising up from the pure-white icing. Everywhere she looked, the touches of the same shades of blue and mauve shone—in the table posies filled with pansies and cornflowers, the bows on the tiny bags of almonds in front of each placemat, and in the bunches of balloons and streamers decorating every corner of the hotel. Claire's and Sophie's dresses also blended perfectly, the colour of the silken fabric enhancing their golden hair and grey eyes.

Ginny grew dreamy, pleasure mingled with the exertions of earlier in the day catching up with her. For a moment, she dropped her chin and closed her eyes, woken seconds later by the scrape of chair legs on the floor.

Tables were being moved to the outer edges of the room. The music started up and Alex and Briony took to the dance floor for their wedding dance.

Kirk sat beside her, his huge hand encompassing hers, then leaned toward her. 'Come on. It's our turn.'

She smiled at him as she rose. The love in his eyes equalled her own and, despite her throbbing feet, she drifted into his arms for a few vague dance steps, barely aware of the crowd growing around them. The volume and rhythm of the music increased—and the party began.

~

AN HOUR LATER, Kirk stepped onto the back veranda of the hotel, frowning at the darkening sky. Although rain had been forecast, the weather bureau assured them it was still a day away. *It appears you are wrong.* Lightning cracked over the hills in the distance and a sickening dread suddenly shot through him, as sudden as a gunshot.

More than a hundred small bales of hay still lay in the paddock, waiting to be stored in the shed. Although the value didn't add up to a fortune, every biscuit of that lucerne was precious. He glanced at his watch. Ten-fifteen. If he slipped out now, he could have the job done and be back before Briony and Alex called it a night and said their goodbyes.

He turned toward the inside of the hotel as the MC announced another bracket of music.

Ginny was leaning forward, smiling as she chatted with Aileen and Bruce. He didn't like to disturb them, but if he waited much longer, he might miss the opportunity of saving the hay.

Brushing a light hand across the back of Ginny's neck, he squatted down so their faces were level and whispered in her ear, 'I'm going to nip home and pop those last bales in the shed. There's a storm coming.'

Concern flashed across Ginny's face, her eyes startled and wide. 'I thought rain wasn't predicted before tomorrow?'

'Yeah, well. You know how it is. The weather is as

unpredictable as the weatherman's forecast.' He chuckled to ease the situation.

'Is everything alright?' Bruce asked, a worried line appearing between his eyebrows.

Ginny flapped a hand, dismissing his concern. 'Everything's fine. Kirk's just going home to put a few things in the shed in case the rain comes early.'

Bruce nodded and reached out a hand to take Ginny's. 'That's grand. While he's away, perhaps you'll dance with me,' he said cheekily.

'And I'll get myself another glass of wine,' Aileen said.

Kirk shot Ginny a grin and slipped quietly out the door.

Having changed his clothes and donned heavy work boots, Kirk charged outside again, his head lowered against the building gale. All around him now, lightning streaked, followed closely by the menacing rumble of thunder.

Deciding to take the farm ute, in which he had left his leather gloves and hay hooks, he leapt in, grabbed the keys from under the passenger seat, and reversed out of the shed.

It took only minutes to reach the bottom paddock where square bales of the precious lucerne lay in neat rows. He shot across the land toward the shed on the far side. Having reversed the hay truck into one bay earlier in the day, leaving the other half of the shed with just enough room for another load, he slowed to a stop in front of the shiny new sliding doors. He had constructed and installed them a year earlier to replace the rotting hinged ones that opened outwards, impeding easy access with the truck. Now, every time he looked at them, a tiny wave of pride filled his chest. Allowing just enough room to slide the massive doors open, he slid out of the driver's seat and strode to the shed.

With the wind howling around his ears, he undid the bolt and slid one hand between the central opening, pressing his chest and other hand against the cold iron, his arms stretched wide.

The gap broadened, the rollers along the top rail shrieking as the door slid. Deafened by the noises surrounding him at every level, Kirk was oblivious to what was happening behind him.

As though arranged by unknown sources, the hairs on the back of his neck rose. Dropping his arms to his sides, he tried to turn around—.

A heavy weight pressed him flat against the door, rods of steel pinning his back and hips against the solid ridges of the bull bar. *I forgot to pull on the handbrake!*

A breath left his body in a slow trickle as the

weight grew heavier. Steeling himself, he raised his arms, pressed his hands against the door, and pushed back against the ute, drawing small, tight breaths, and filling his lungs to capacity. But there was not a skerrick of wiggle room.

Nausea rose in his stomach before he realised the vehicle was stationary. He tried to move, inching a little to the right and left, but, with the ute on a slightly downhill angle, he had no hope of moving the two-tonne vehicle. A stab of fury swept through him. *If I could just bend my knees, I might have a chance of moving it enough to wriggle free.* But his lower back and legs were firmly pinned, and there was nothing he could do to release them. Anger turned to despair as the first spits of rain hit him. Within seconds, fat drops hammered on the roof before, goaded by the wind, they whipped around the side of the shed and soaked him to the skin.

He bowed his head, leaning his forehead against the door, and closed his eyes. Trapped, all he could do was remain calm and brace himself against the ute, desperately praying it wouldn't roll any farther while he thought of Ginny and hoped she would come looking for him.

~

PERSPIRATION POURED in a rivulet down Ginny's back. With a friendly shove, she pushed Sam away from her.

'That's me done. Sorry. My feet are killing me. You'll have to find another partner.'

Sam's face lit up with a smile. Tucking her hand into his elbow, he escorted her to a table where Eleanor and Lola were sipping tea.

Ginny slumped in the chair and gave Sam a smile of gratitude. 'Thanks, Sam. You've been very kind.' Waving to Sophie, who was one-handedly stacking glasses on a tray, she added, 'You'd better rescue Soph now. She seems to have forgotten she's a bridesmaid tonight and bridesmaids do not have to clean up after everyone.'

Sam retreated with a wide grin on his face.

'I don't know how you do it, Ginny,' Lola said. 'Even when I was your age, I don't think I could have danced more than one bracket.'

'Phew.' She released a heated breath and dabbed her face with the serviette. 'It's been a while since I danced as much as I have tonight. Don't you worry, I'll pay for it tomorrow.'

They laughed, and Ginny downed a glass of water before glancing at her watch.

'Kirk's not back yet, is he?'

Both Lola and Eleanor shook their heads. 'I haven't seen him,' Eleanor said.

'Maybe he's out the back talking with some of the

other men. I think it got a bit noisy in here, so they took their drinks and ambled outside a while ago. Probably wanted to watch the rain come in,' Lola added.

Ginny checked her watch again, then dug her phone out of her evening purse and frowned. 'He's been gone almost two hours and there's no message from him. It's not like him to do that.' She swept her gaze around the room as Lola rose to her feet.

'I'll check with the fellas.'

'It looks like Briony and Alex are doing the rounds of saying goodbye to guests,' Eleanor said, flicking a hand toward the opposite side of the room.

As if sensing their eyes on her, Briony looked across at her mother, a small frown playing on her face. She touched Alex's shoulder lightly before heading towards them.

'Everything alright? You're worried our presence is preventing guests from going home, aren't you?'

'No, love. It's not always the done thing, but I think most people who needed to, have already said goodbye and gone.' She drew a deep breath. 'No, I'm worried about Kirk. He went home to get the last of the hay in the shed before the rain and hasn't returned.'

Briony's eyebrows shot up. 'How long ago?'

'Almost two hours.'

'Oh. Should we send Frank and a couple of the men to check?'

Ginny met her daughter's worried stare. 'Yes, perhaps that's a good idea. I'll go with them. It's probably nothing. Maybe the truck wouldn't start—you know how it can play up sometimes, especially when we need it most.'

She forced a weak smile on her face and attempted to swallow the lump in her throat. 'I shouldn't have let him go alone. I'm sure Rhys would have been happy to give him a hand.'

At that moment, both Claire and Rhys appeared at her side with Lola, Frank, Bruce, and a few others trailing behind them.

'She's pouring out there now!' Bruce said cheerfully. 'Looks like Scotland—except it's about twenty degrees hotter.'

As though suddenly registering the serious expressions on everyone's face, his smile faded. 'Something up?'

'Could be,' Rhys said in an authoritative tone. 'Kirk hasn't returned, so a couple of us are going to check on him.' He turned to Claire and rested a hand on her shoulder. 'Might be an idea if you ask the DJ to finish up now, and Briony and Sophie can go around and thank everyone for coming. I'll ask Mark to close the bar. That way, most will get the hint the night is over.'

As they gave murmurs and nods of approval, he added, 'Be subtle! We don't want to make a fuss if there's nothing wrong and Kirk's just fallen asleep or something.'

Ginny met his gaze, and her heart shuddered. The wariness in his eyes did not match his reassuring words.

There's no way Kirk would be asleep. Something is wrong.

29

The surprisingly rapid finish to Briony and Alex's wedding celebrations drew a worried frown from Eleanor as her and Francene's eyes met.

Francene crossed the room and sat beside her friend. 'What's going on? Briony and Alex seem to be bothered about something?'

Eleanor rested a hand on Francene's. 'I'm sure everything is fine. It appears Kirk hasn't returned from the farm. He dashed home to rescue a truckload of hay before it got wet, and I guess the storm has added difficulties he didn't expect. Whatever it is, Ginny and Rhys have gone to check on him and Briony and Alex are ready to call it a day here so they're saying goodbye to their guests and hope they take the hint.'

They sat in silence for a full minute before Eleanor asked, 'How did everything go in the kitchen?'

'Fabulous. Ann was organised and somehow managed to supervise the wait staff to ensure everything went smoothly.' Strands of hair had fallen from her elastic tie, and she tucked them behind her ears. 'The kitchen is spotless again and the helpers have gone home.'

'I thought Mark and Ann would have been guests today, not workers,' Eleanor said, voicing Francene's thoughts.

She looked at the older woman and shrugged. 'I admit I thought the same, but Ann told me they considered the best wedding present they could give Briony and Alex was to be in charge of the bar and catering. That way everyone was happy.'

Eleanor nodded her approval. 'They certainly did a wonderful job—as did you.' She squeezed Francene's hand again. 'Those canapes were absolutely delicious, and the petit fours and cake were magnificent. I'm sure not one person would have gone home disappointed, and you'll be busier than you think once your tearoom is up and running.'

A warm glow filled Francene. Although weary, she had revelled in the excitement and stimulation the day's event had provided. Hers had begun at dawn, the early morning walk and pot of tea ensuring she'd had a refreshing start. Having a practice run earlier in the week then cooking in the hotel's well-equipped kitchen, she had loved working alongside Ann and Sophie and Alex's parents—to the point where she and Ann had almost had to force Aileen and Bruce upstairs to get ready for the wedding.

While she'd focused on the final touches of her creations, Francene's mind drifted to plans for "Tea, Tarts and Treasures". There was only one week before Christmas, but while she waited to hear from the council about her licencing requirements, she'd scrubbed the little house from top to bottom the minute Pam handed her the keys. Time spent in the cottage on her own would show her its soul and would also give her time to paint the interior walls and consider how she would furnish the rooms. Amongst the items she had gathered since Kyle's death was an antique brass bedhead she'd picked up at a garage sale for fifty dollars. Together with the chunky but beautifully polished dressing table she'd rescued from her grandmother's home and the patchwork quilt her mother had made her for her twentieth birthday— which Kyle had hated so she'd hidden it away in a cupboard and accepted the hideous black and white bedspread he'd insisted they use—her new bedroom would be exactly the way she wanted it. She would keep an eye out for a comfortable second-hand sofa— and together with the kitchen table and wardrobes already in the house, she would have everything she needed except a bed.

First thing on Monday, I'll buy myself a new one—and have a look for suitable tables and chairs for my business.

Eleanor jumped as a deafening thunderclap sounded above them, bringing Francene's wanderings to the present.

'Yikes. I don't like the sound of that,' Eleanor said. 'Wherever he is, I hope Kirk is safe and dry.'

Francene raised an eyebrow. She'd never experienced a cyclone but didn't mind storms, provided they weren't destructive. Rather, she enjoyed watching them exert their power, growling and blowing like a furious beast or, better still, lying in bed with the curtains open so she could see the changes in light and the thrashing of rain against the windows. 'Me too.'

She touched Eleanor's arm lightly. 'I think it's time I headed to bed.'

Eleanor released a tired sigh. 'You're right. There's nothing we can do to help here now. Sam and his helpers have done a wonderful job, so I'll come upstairs with you.'

As the two women trod slowly up the carpeted staircase, another golden flash lit up the entire hotel. They paused and Francene counted aloud. 'One, two, three …' Then a deafening crash of thunder followed.

Eleanor clutched Francene's wrist. 'This is bad.'

Suddenly Francene's thoughts flew from watching the storm rage from her warm and dry bedroom to Ginny and Rhys driving around in the pouring rain looking for Kirk. A knot formed in her stomach as the women faced each other. She couldn't speak. This wasn't about the storm. *Something more serious has happened.*

BRYN LEANED against the veranda railing, marvelling at the changing colours in the sky as the showers morphed from thick, grey clouds to torrential white sheets that buffeted the trees and stripped many of their leaves.

Alternate shards of bright lightning split the air, closely followed by increasingly deafening thunder.

His hip ached as he watched. *My fault for spending too long at the workbench.*

He'd vaguely heard the line of vehicles coming and going from Featherwood Station as he worked during the day and hoped Briony's wedding had gone to plan.

He was about to turn and retreat inside when another flash of lightning lit up the sky, sending a yellow glow over the valley. As the oak tree in the front garden swayed in the gale, he glimpsed the old hay shed in a paddock near the Featherwood Station woolshed. Early that morning, the rumble of a hay baler had woken him and he had risen, astounded to see the green tractor circumnavigating the lucerne paddock. *On their daughter's wedding day?*

He'd chuckled to himself, recalling the number of times he'd heard his mother complain about his father *having* to finish planting or harvesting a crop, or shifting a mob of sheep at the last minute and making the family late to whatever event they were supposed to attend. That's farming, he'd said to no one, his mind revisiting the thought of rescuing a dog for company.

His eyes narrowed at the sight of the farm ute outside the shed. Hurrying inside, he snatched up the binoculars he'd bought in Stanthorpe to better study the birds he liked to carve. Then, back on the veranda, he focused on the shed and adjusted the zoom.

Dropping the binoculars from his face, he focused again on the hay shed before lifting the glasses and taking another, more thorough look. Choking back a gasp, he froze. He wasn't imagining things—between the shed door and the front of the utility, someone stood motionless as though fixed to the iron.

Horror filled him—the nightmare that had plagued him for years following a moving tractor pinning his best friend against a building, causing him to lose his life, swallowed him.

For several moments, he couldn't move. Then, galvanised into action, he thundered inside, dropped the binoculars on the couch, and snatched his coat and hat off the hook beside the door. In seconds, he was reversing his ute out of the shed and accelerating up the rise to the farm gate.

An involuntary 'No!' exploded from him as he drove into the lucerne paddock, the outline of Kirk's bulky frame now visible.

Easing to a stop near the shed, he peered through the teaming rain, threw the driver's door open, and ran. All thoughts of his aching hip and back disappeared as he sprinted to Kirk.

'Kirk! It's me. Bryn. Are you alright, mate?'

Despite Bryn's shout, there was no movement from the big man. Pressing against the bar that had Kirk pinned, Bryn reached over and placed his fingers against Kirk's bearded throat.

Kirk adjusted his head, meeting Bryn's eyes, and whispered, 'Could be better.'

A flood of relief swept through Bryn. Snatching his phone from his pocket, he moved away from the shed, aware of the intermittent signal, and dialled triple zero.

The wait seemed interminable as the operator questioned him then switched him to the correct department.

'Ambulance. How can I help you?'

In a rush, Bryn shared the address, Kirk's name, and the situation. The calm but professional voice of the respondent requested further details while reassuring Bryn he was connecting the call to the ambulance service closest to the farm.

'Please stay on the line,' he said. 'We have paramedics on their way—however, it could take up to thirty minutes for them to reach you.'

Bryn's shoulders sagged as he digested this information, memories of his own accident flashing before his eyes, and he swallowed the bile that surged to his throat. 'Hang on a second while I put you on speaker.'

Bryn stared into the pelting rain, his heart pounding like a runaway horse as he moved next to Kirk and tried to focus on the questions he was being asked.

'Okay. Is the patient conscious and able to talk?'

'Yes, a little. He's freezing—and soaked to the skin. We're in the middle of a storm here.'

'Hmm. Can he move at all?'

Bryn repeated the question to Kirk, leaning closer to listen to his whispered answers.

'Yeah. His arms are free and he can lift them. He's been trying to shuffle his feet, but he's too tightly jammed to bend his knees or flex in any direction.'

'Okay. Can you get him to hold the bull bar and use it as a prop while you move the vehicle away from the shed?'

Bryn met Kirk's eyes enquiringly. Nodding, Kirk slowly reached back, hooking his arms over the bull bar. Bryn slid into the vehicle, his foot firmly on the foot brake as he turned the key. The engine roared into life and slowly, with his pulse pounding in his ears, he reversed centimetre by centimetre until he'd gained enough space between the ute and shed to manoeuvre Kirk away from the building and in to shelter. Then he hauled the hand-brake on, switched off the engine, and leapt out.

'Righto. He's still upright and hanging on to the bull bar. I reckon I can get him inside the hay shed if that's okay?'

'Well done. Yes, no need to take him too far until he's been checked out. If you can, lie him down and keep him warm.'

Accompanied by a series of groans and sharp breaths, Bryn eased Kirk's arm around his shoulder while wrapping his own around Kirk's waist. Then, with a slow, measured shuffle, they tottered into the shed before both slumping in a heap on a layer of hay bales. While Bryn stripped off his coat and shirt, Kirk eased himself onto his back and obediently allowed Bryn to tuck his rolled-up shirt under Kirk's neck and spread the dry inside of the coat over the top of him.

Pressing the phone against his ear again, Bryn relayed the information to the paramedic seconds before the headlights of a vehicle appeared, roaring along the track toward him. Almost collapsing with relief, Bryn shouted down the phone, 'Help has arrived!'

Rhys and Ginny leapt out and rushed toward them. Seemingly oblivious to her stylish bronze-coloured dress being immediately soaked and the fine material gluing itself to her body, Ginny ran straight to Kirk while Rhys appeared at Bryn's elbow.

'Sergeant Rhys Morton here. What's the situation with the ambo?'

'It'll be a while, but please stay on the line.'

He repeated many of the questions he had asked Bryn again, clearly requiring a constant situation report as the thunder clapped around them and the rain pelted the shed roof with a deafening staccato.

After what seemed like hours but was only twenty minutes, the faint sound of a siren drew closer, the strobing blue and red lights competing with sheet lightning as the ambulance slowed, turned into the Featherwood Station driveway, and proceeded carefully across the increasingly muddy paddock.

After a thorough examination, Kirk was loaded onto a gurney and lifted into the ambulance. Ginny clambered in after him, reassured by Rhys that he and Claire would be not far behind them and would bring dry clothing for her, while Bryn stood, wrapped in the blanket Rhys had hauled out of the police car, desperately trying to hide his shaking limbs.

A rapid exchange of information between Rhys and Claire on the phone followed, arrangements were made, and in less than a minute, Rhys was resting his hand on Bryn's shoulder. 'Thanks, mate. Really appreciate your help. Leave your ute here and let me drop you home. You need a warm shower and a hot cup of tea.'

Bryn nodded and trailed behind as Rhys strode toward his vehicle.

With Bryn standing under the beam of light streaming from his back porch, Rhys yelled, 'I'll call you with an update,' and drove away.

Relieved to be alone again, Bryn gave in to his jelly-like legs, staggered inside, and collapsed on a kitchen chair. With his back bent, he held his head in his hands, reliving both his own and Kirk's accidents, the flashes of horror and disbelief rendering him immobile. His body continued to shake until eventually, he dragged himself to his feet, his hip screaming with pain as he shuffled his way to the bathroom.

30

It was after midnight when Rhys called to advise Kirk was stable but would remain in the hospital for further tests and observation. Although the early prognosis appeared satisfactory, Rhys explained they were concerned about a condition called Rhabdomyolysis, commonly termed *Rhabdo* —muscle damage which was often caused by a crush injury.

'The doctor said his muscular physique and size probably saved him from further injuries, and if he'd been facing the ute instead of the shed, he probably would have been able to push the ute off himself,' Rhys added.

Bryn's heart ached for the gigantic, kind man who had gone out of his way to supply Bryn with the perfect timber for his creations. It still seemed incredible that he had survived the ordeal and Bryn understood more than most that no accident passed without some hardships. Kirk would likely have more than just physical injuries to recover from. By the time he'd been freed, he had been immobilised with half his body compressed between the wall and bull bar for over two hours.

Following Rhys's call, Bryn lay on the sofa, listening to the storm soften and move away into the distance. The painkillers he'd taken earlier finally kicked in and once again he felt in control of his body —*probably more than poor Kirk does at the moment.* Then, warmed by a mug of hot, sweet chocolate and the alpaca rug Mae had given him the previous Christmas, he wandered down the hallway to the safety of his bed.

As with most stormy nights, the following morning dawned clear and bright, the dazzling light causing Bryn's eyes to water as he strolled onto the front veranda with a mug of coffee in his hand.

After the trauma of the previous night, he hadn't expected to sleep, but he had—heavily. Despite the exertion he had put his body through, he was surprised to admit he felt more rejuvenated than he had in a long time. It had been more than two years since he had sprinted anywhere, and yet he had no more pain than usual. *Perhaps I should restart my fitness regime instead of just following the physio program?*

At the sound of a vehicle approaching, he craned his neck to look through the torn leaves of the oak tree, grinning to himself. For someone who was seeking privacy, he quite enjoyed noting the vehicles that drove past. Except for the residents and visitors to Featherwood Station, only a few white utes with the Queensland Forestry emblem on the doors used the road. He presumed they were taking a back track he was yet unaware of in order to reach one of the vast blocks of forestry planted haphazardly around the ridges. His interest piqued as a small silver car crept along the gravel, closely followed by a red SUV. He was even more surprised when both vehicles slowed and then turned into his driveway.

For a second, he glanced down at his bare feet and baggy shorts and considered finding a pair of shoes before walking out to greet them. Too late, Eleanor, the mature-aged woman he'd met at Ginny and Kirk's wedding celebration, stepped out of the small car, followed by Francene in the older SUV.

He blinked hard, his heart taking a momentary leap of unexpected delight.

After stepping carefully down the stairs, he crossed the wet grass while the women raised the rear door of

Eleanor's car and Francene reached into its depths and removed a box.

'Good morning,' he called.

Eleanor snapped to attention and strode toward him, a friendly smile spreading across her face. She held out her hand and he took it gently, surprised at her firm grip.

'Good morning, Bryn.' She gave a vague wave toward Francene, who waited with the box in her arms. 'Francene's got something for you.'

He nodded and threw Francene a grin. 'Gidday.'

'You're probably wondering why we're here,' Eleanor continued. 'As you know, it was Briony and Alex's wedding yesterday and I believe you had an interrupted night assisting with Kirk's awful accident.' She raised an eyebrow as though expecting his confirmation.

'Um, yes. I gave him a hand.'

'A timely one by all accounts. And that's why we've got a few bits and pieces from the wedding for you.'

Now totally miffed, he frowned, shaking his head. He didn't need gifts—or charity.

Francene stepped closer to him and held out the box. 'Here. We kind of over-catered and thought you might enjoy a piece of the wedding cake and ... a few other items.'

He took the box from her, his hand touching hers.

Instant heat radiated through him as colour crept into his face.

'I'm not starving,' he said, immediately regretting his words as he read her mortified expression. 'I'm sorry, I meant that as a joke.'

She gave him a wobbly smile, as if she didn't believe him but was prepared to let it go.

'Of course you're not,' Eleanor said firmly. 'It's just there's a lot going on at the moment ... Alex and Briony are about to head off with Alex's parents for a few days at the coast, leaving Claire helping Mark and Ann at the hotel as well as the farm. Ginny is staying in town while Kirk's in hospital, and ...' She paused for a moment and Francene intervened.

'We offered to stay at the farm and care for the animals while Ginny and Kirk are away. Claire will be here soon to show us the routine, and by way of thanks for your quick thinking and help last night, we thought you might appreciate a change from whatever it is you usually cook and enjoy some leftovers.'

Their eyes held as he read her uncertainty.

Bryn relaxed, his smile widening. 'Thank you. It's very kind ... and yes, I admit while I don't mind cooking, I live pretty simply—but I do alright for myself.'

They all laughed, the colour in Francene's cheeks matching his own. As though needing the distraction as much as he did, she pointed to the various containers in the box. 'There are a few savouries in there—I made too many,' she said apologetically. 'And that one's got a piece of wedding cake in it. I'm guessing you don't bake cakes very often?'

He shook his head. 'Definitely not. Eat them, yes. Bake them, no.'

'Okay. Well, I hope you enjoy it.'

Oblivious to Eleanor's amused smile, Bryn and Francene's eyes remained fixed on each other, the lengthy pause suggesting an invisible connection between them.

Bryn jerked, snapping back to the present. 'I can help with the feeding routine if you like. I stayed there for a while before I moved here—and although I didn't do any farm work, I often watched as Kirk or Ginny carried out their daily chores.' He stopped, squirming at his own suggestion of laziness. 'I grew up on the land, you see, so it's kind of second nature,' he gabbled.

He could almost hear their relieved breaths as both women looked at each other.

'Thanks, Bryn. We would welcome any help or advice you can give us,' Eleanor said. 'I'll be staying until Ginny no longer needs me, but Francene needs to be at her house on Tuesday for the removal company.'

Bryn's eyebrows shot up. 'You're moving in already?'

'Yes. A short settlement period and the guys from the removal company were happy to fit me in as a back load. Apparently, they're delivering furniture to Brisbane this weekend and then want to return to Sydney before Christmas. Seemed sensible for them to drop my stuff off on their way—cheaper for me too,' Francene added.

An unfamiliar sense of hope soared inside him. 'Happy to give you a hand if you need it,' he said.

Her mouth quirked as their eyes met again. 'Thanks. The removal guys will probably do the heavy lifting—but if I need you, I'll call.'

Burning with optimism, he placed the box carefully on the ground at his feet, pulled his phone out of his pocket, and looked at Francene. 'I'll send you a text so you've got my number.'

After a slight pause, Francene nodded and shared her details, watching as he punched it in his phone and they waited for the vibration, signalling connectivity.

Then, with a brief wave, the women returned to their vehicles, leaving Bryn holding his boxes of delicacies.

As Eleanor drove past him wearing a knowing smile, he huffed, wondering what on earth had instigated his attraction to Francene. He'd come here to recuperate and start a new life. Previous girlfriends had been just that—young, fun, and fleeting—and had no place in his future. But Francene was different, and he couldn't help feeling something more than just being interested.

I wonder if she feels the same as I do.

31

Ginny paced up and down the corridor, unable to sit a moment longer.

Blood tests and X-rays had established nothing was out of the ordinary with Kirk, however the doctor wanted to keep him in hospital for another night to be certain. Exhaustion seemed to have settled over him, and Ginny was a little concerned at his ability to fall asleep regardless of what was going on around him. On the contrary, she was wired, the adrenaline still pulsing through her veins as she reflected on the whole terrifying incident.

A choking sob caught in her throat again, and she straightened her shoulders and drew a deep breath. Kirk did not need her falling to pieces. *Get your act together.* For the second time that morning, she marched through the front foyer of the hospital and outside into the fresh air. Then, swiping her phone, she tapped the screen and waited for Briony to answer.

'Hi, Mum. How's Kirk?'

'Sleeping. The test results have come back normal, so hopefully we'll both be home tomorrow.'

'Great! That's good news.' Briony's relieved breath sounded in Ginny's ear. 'Before you ask, the car is packed, Claire is here with both Mark and Ann, and we're only minutes away from heading off.'

'Super. Did Claire give Eleanor and Francene instructions for animal feeding? And are they okay to stay overnight?' Ginny's thoughts leapt from one thing to the next. 'Lucky I put clean sheets on both spare beds before the wedding. I half thought we may have had someone staying over—but I never dreamed it would be in these circumstances.'

Briony's calm tones penetrated her scattered brain. 'Yes to everything. Mum, you don't need to worry. It's only for a couple of days and Bryn has also offered to help. He and Francene will check the troughs and feed the horses and dogs. Eleanor's a cat lover so will take care of them—and your precious hens. Lola and Frank said they'd come, but I've assured them it's under control.' Her voice lowered a notch. 'When I popped in to drop off Lola's cake containers and some of the left-over food, they both looked tired and were minding a bawling Liam while Emma was giving a music lesson and Ryan took the rubbish to the tip. They think Liam's teething.'

The hint of a smile hovered on Ginny's mouth as she pictured Briony's eye roll. Although Briony never commented, it was clear she felt Ryan and Emma smothered more love and attention on their adored son than was normal. Her attitude had surprised Ginny, as both her daughters had been devoted and loving toward their pets and she was sure they would be no different if and when they had children. But Briony's strong business head and love of routine conflicted with the confused realisation that babies didn't always operate by the clock or the rule book. *Your turn will come.* She smiled.

'I hope Aileen and Bruce enjoy Yamba.'

'Oh, they will. We'll stop frequently on the journey too, so they have time to explore our lovely beaches.'

They continued chatting for a few minutes before ending the call.

While she waited for the elevator, Ginny reflected on the news that Bryn was helping at the farm and he and Francene were working together. Intrigue mixed with relief and, as the elevator doors opened and she stepped inside, the last of the adrenaline faded and a wave of fatigue washed over her. Perhaps she would snaffle one of Kirk's pillows and drag the chair up against his bed so she could rest her head close to his and get some much-needed sleep.

With that thought in mind, she hurried along the hallway, desperate to wrap her arms around her precious husband.

BRYN CAST a sideways glance at Francene as she bucketed the grotty green water from the bottom of the trough. He was pleased he'd come. As luck would have it, it appeared the moment Ginny and Kirk were away from the place, the cattle found other ways to occupy themselves besides eating, drinking, and sleeping. Whatever game the youngsters were playing, the carefully attached protective cage that would normally cover the float valve, preventing damage to the interruption of water flow, had been bent out of shape, allowing something solid to snap the arm of the float valve. The water had stopped flowing and the trough held only a fraction of what it should.

'Does this sort of thing happen often?' Francene asked.

'Not really. But wherever you have strong, healthy stock, I guess you have to expect a bit of rough treatment from time to time. We had a pony when I was a kid that loved to paddle in the troughs. He would get in and paw the water until he'd emptied most of it—and often smashed the float valve and its protective basket. We ended up having to put a row of heavy posts across all the troughs in the paddocks that held cattle and horses. Sheep are more gentle, so it's not such an issue.'

Francene smiled at him. 'I think I might be more of a sheep person then.'

He raised an eyebrow. Her nonchalant attitude to the dirty work and smells, and her sensible, accepting manner of all things farm-related, staggered him. 'I thought you were a townie?'

'I am, really. But years ago I had a friend with grandparents who farmed, and we stayed with them a bit during the school holidays. I loved it.'

'But not enough to encourage you to consider working in agriculture?'

She shook her head. 'No. My parents were teachers and wanted me to follow in their footsteps. But I've always loved cooking, especially making decorative cakes and stuff like that.' She stood up, her eyes holding a faraway look in them for a moment. 'I was in the city one day just before I finished my final year in school and I walked past a patisserie. The smell of the food was amazing, and I went in. I bought a religieuse and it melted in my mouth.'

'What on earth is a religieuse?'

She chuckled, dropping the bucket beside the now-empty trough. 'One of my parents' favourite treats.

They met in France, you see? My mother is French, and that's why they wanted to go back there. Religieuse are a pretty common French dessert. They're made with two choux pastry buns on top of each other—the bottom one is larger and fatter and the top one is round and small—so they kind of look like a chubby nun. The chocolate over the top makes the habit around her shoulders. It's all filled with cream or custard and topped with chocolate icing. So good.'

'Sounds delicious. So, carry on. What happened next?' Although they had touched on previous employment during their morning-tea date, she had simply mentioned she worked in a bakery before switching to office work.

'I asked if they needed anyone over the school holidays—and they did. Accepted me after only a few minutes of discussion.'

'How did your parents feel about that?' Bryn took a step back from the repaired float valve and gave it a gentle push. Clean water flowed out as Francene continued.

'They weren't happy. But ... I was determined, and when Henry offered me an apprenticeship as a pastry chef, I jumped at it.'

'And you've worked there until now?'

Her shoulders slumped and for a moment, he cringed. *I'm being too nosey.*

'No. About ten years ago, I got married. My

husband didn't like me working the weird hours, so I changed to office work.'

'I see.' He spoke slowly, not seeing much at all except what an idiot her husband must be, allowing a talent like hers to be wasted. A spear of anxiety stabbed him. 'Is he joining you here?'

She shook her head firmly. 'No. He died. In a car crash earlier in the year.'

'I'm sorry for asking. I didn't mean to upset you.'

Facing him with a determined, clear-eyed stare, she grunted. 'You're not. Upsetting me, I mean. When we married, I knew nothing about personality disorders or coercive control, not to mention gambling habits.'

Her voice had such a bitter tone to it, he almost stepped back.

'He had all of those and despite a million red flags, it took me a ridiculously long time to realise it. By then he'd gambled every cent we had in our joint account and all my friends had scarpered. I wasn't well and my doctor sent me for counselling. Lucky, really. The counsellor was lovely and incredibly kind. She loaned me a book to read about narcissism, and I got a shock. It was like reading Kyle's biography.' She drew another deep breath without her eyes leaving his. 'Anyway, I started a bank account of my own and carefully began moving some of my most precious personal items into a box I hid under the spare bed. He did no housework, so was unlikely to look there. But then I came home one day to discover he'd sold our lovely dining suite and used the money to gamble—unsuccessfully. I was furious but too frightened to do anything. We barely spoke for a week. Then, as usual, he went out on Friday night and never came back. About two o'clock in the morning, the police knocked on our door and told me he'd been killed.'

Bryn rocked on his feet, his eyes wide with horror, itching to wrap her in a big hug. 'I'm so sorry, Francene.'

'Don't be. It's good to unload some of that stuff, actually. The only other person who knows everything is Eleanor. She's been such a wonderful friend, despite our age difference.'

He nodded then bent down to pick up the bucket and tools he'd found in the toolbox on the ute tray.

'Next paddock?' Francene asked.

'Yep. Hopefully that's our problems sorted for the day.' He shot her a warm smile.

Almost half an hour passed with only a few words shared before they completed the round of the troughs and headed toward the homestead.

'I meant what I said about helping with your new house, Francene. I know I look a bit beat up, but I'm quite strong.'

He grinned as she glanced at his legs.

'What happened? You've heard my story. Now it's your turn.'

'You really want to know?'

'I reckon it's only fair, don't you?'

'I suppose so.' He shrugged. At least he hadn't had relationship problems, and now he knew what she'd been through, he hoped she would understand.

'I fell off a roof.'

She stared at him wide-eyed. 'And?'

'I worked for a construction company as a roofer. That is a person who puts roofs on houses.'

'I think I understand what a roofer might do,' she said with a touch of amused sarcasm.

'Of course, sorry.' He hesitated for a second, a little surprised that Claire had obviously not shared the information he had already given. Perhaps the bush telegraph wasn't quite as strong as he'd thought? Or perhaps these lovely people were more respectful than he had become used to.

Giving a tiny shrug, he continued. 'Didn't end well. I don't remember much of the actual fall, except trying to grab the scaffolding as I went over the edge and realising it hadn't been screwed in properly.' He glanced at her worried frown. 'It was one of those situations none of us think will be a problem. We were under pressure to get the roof on as a storm was predicted. So, we started working before the scaffolding guys had finished—totally against the rules. Then, of course, yours truly, who's usually fairly nimble-footed, makes a tiny mistake while reaching for the next sheet of iron as a gust of wind blew ... and everything happened.'

'You're lucky to still be alive,' Francene said, her voice high with astonishment. 'So how badly hurt were you?'

'Broken back, pelvis, and leg. Luckily the back mended—well, everything did eventually, thanks to a heap of plates and pins and a team of excellent surgeons. When they first told me about my back, I remember thinking I'd rather die than be in a wheelchair. But someone was on my side and two years later, here I am.'

They pulled into the farm vehicle shed as he finished, switching off the engine and sitting in silence for a moment.

Francene opened the door and slid out before walking around to his side and waiting for him. As his feet hit the ground, she said, 'Thank you for sharing that with me.'

'Thanks for listening.'

'Can I give you a hug?'

Her question came with such surprise, his jaw dropped, then he shut his mouth before opening his arms.

She wrapped hers around him, leaning against his shoulder as he clasped her tightly and pressed his face against her thick, shiny hair. It smelled clean and fresh, despite having been exposed to all things farm-related.

Her slim body sent a quiver of emotion through him—one he hadn't experienced for a long time—and a warm flush of joy, comradeship, and something he didn't recognise surged through him.

He didn't want to let her go, and from the strength of her hug, he enjoyed a strong suspicion she felt the same.

32

———

$\mathcal{A}$ tiny wave of regret swept through Bryn as he watched Claire's car drive past his house with Ginny in the driver's seat and Kirk next to her. Although relieved Kirk didn't have any significant injuries and had already been discharged from the hospital, Bryn had enjoyed his two days helping on their farm, especially with Francene beside him.

There was something about her he couldn't put his finger on but knew it was positive. Despite what must have been a rocky and at times terrifying relationship with her husband, her initial reticence had diminished, and in each other's company, he felt only companionship, warmth, and a spark of a stronger emotion.

Perhaps it's living here.

Although Francene appeared quiet and introverted, her earlier reluctance to converse with him had also vanished and that morning while driving around checking the troughs, she had seemed relaxed, talking almost constantly in a friendly, interested way. Covering common topics like the weather and beauty of the countryside, their conversation had delved more deeply into their previous jobs, books, movies, and Bryn's experiences while working in England as a carpenter.

As though both were dancing around unresolved issues, the one thing not discussed had been their families. Bryn considered the relationship between him and his parents and brothers to be difficult, and he wasn't ready to share details. Hearing Francene's revelation of living with a coercive and manipulating personality, he had been shocked to link her deceased husband's similarities with his own father. It had been on the tip of his tongue to delve further, but he hadn't. Instead, his heart had filled with empathy and understanding.

His phone vibrated in his pocket, jolting him from his thoughts. He dragged it out, his heart leaping as Francene's name appeared on the screen.

'Hi.'

'Hi, Bryn.'

There was a pause, and he heard the inward drawing of breath, as though she wasn't sure what to say—or was hesitant to say it.

'Everything alright?' he said. 'Did the removal truck arrive this morning?'

'Eventually. They didn't get here until late—which was probably not a bad thing as I got all the walls and floors washed.'

'So, is everything in its place or do you need a hand?'

'Yes please. That's why I was ringing, really. Would you have half an hour to help me put furniture into place? The removal guys were okay, but they pretty much just dumped everything in the middle of the rooms, and I don't want to scratch the lovely floors. It looks like they were only resurfaced recently.'

A surge of pleasure burst into his chest. 'I'll come down now if that's okay.'

'Thanks heaps.'

They ended the call, and Bryn shoved his feet into a pair of sneakers and grabbed his keys.

For a second, he stared at the walking stick leaning in the corner and grunted. 'You can stay right where you are,' he said crisply.

Even when the pain hit with unexpected force, at times threatening to topple him over, he had been persistent, determined to be independent of artificial support by Christmas.

He walked along the path leading to Francene's cute cottage with barely a limp and joyous anticipation in his heart.

The door was wide open, and music drifted out to meet him.

'Hello!' he called.

Francene hurried toward him from the far end of the house.

'Hi there. I've been unpacking the boxes of kitchen stuff—there's a lot!'

He grinned, momentarily glued to the strands of dark hair hanging around her face and restraining himself from reaching out and tucking them behind her ears.

Then, casting his eyes around the front room, he observed slight marks on the floor. *Where an adjoining wall used to be.* It was clear the front portion of the original hallway was now encompassed into a large, airy space with French doors leading onto the front veranda.

'Is this going to be the tearoom?'

'Yes. That and the veranda, which will be nice most of the year. Come in and I'll show you around.'

Opening the first door on his left, she stood back and waved Bryn inside. His eyebrows lifted at the solid timber desk with beautifully carved legs and a leather top. Boxes were stacked on the floor beside it and a printer with its cord trailing across the floor sat beneath it.

'Your office.'

'Yes. And probably where I'll keep the stock for my

shop—you know, gifts and things like that. I'd like to buy another wardrobe or something similar, so I can keep the room tidy. After all, there's not only the doors for people to look through but also the side window— and it will be my private house. If the business grows enough to need the space, I'll use the room off the front veranda. It's rather small and I plan to store tables and chairs there, but if I have to, it can also double as a storeroom for gifts.'

'Good idea.' He turned, and their eyes met. 'Have you received permission to go ahead with your tearoom?'

She shook her head. 'Not yet, but the council guy couldn't see any reason for it not being approved. There will be conditions—one of which will to have toilet facilities built out the back. I plan on upgrading the kitchen benches and shelving for compliance too, but otherwise, everything is ready to go.'

Her eyes sparkled with excitement.

'Okay then. Where do you want to start?' he said.

'The bedroom.'

For a second he froze, his eyes wide. Then he grinned. 'Sure.'

Oblivious, or ignoring his reaction, Francene walked to the next door leading from the small passageway to the rear of the house before throwing it open.

A brand-new, queen-sized bed sat in the middle of

the room, the mattress still in its protective plastic wrap, and a beautiful dressing table complete with a fluted-edged mirror and antique handles rested next to the wardrobe.

'Nice,' Bryn said, his eyes roving admiringly over the dresser.

'It was my great-grandmother's—the one I told you about,' Francene explained. 'It sat under Mum and Dad's house for years and as they didn't want it, I planned to have it restored when I got married. But it stayed in our garage with a blanket over it for years and somehow the restoration never happened. After Kyle died, one of the antique shops recommended a man who enjoyed doing up old furniture as a hobby. He arranged for it to be collected, had it for about two months, and then delivered it back to me, complete with this gorgeous shellack coating.' She ran her hand over the smooth surface, as if unable to believe her luck. 'It was around the same time I received the repossession notice from the bank for our house so everything I had was put straight into storage, including this.' She waved a hand around. 'It's been months since most of these boxes were packed, so I'm not exactly certain what's in them now.'

'It'll be like Christmas for you then,' he chuckled.

'Yeah.' She shrugged. 'I plan to have another shopping trip to Warwick or Stanthorpe over the next couple of weeks to get shelving and whatever else I need. Shame the council close for two weeks, but I'll just have to be patient and hope they don't reject my application.'

'Speaking of Christmas, what are you doing over the break?'

'Ginny and Kirk invited Eleanor and me to their place for Christmas Day. That was before the accident though, so I'm not sure if the invitation still stands. Other than that, I reckon I'll have my hands full here, getting organised. What about you?'

He rolled his eyes. 'Promised my mother I'd go home.'

For a few seconds, an awkward silence hung in the air.

'And you don't want to?'

His shoulders slumped. 'It's not that. It-it's complicated. Dad will control every conversation from the moment I step out of the car—like he always does. And Owen, my eldest brother, and his bossy wife and wild, undisciplined kids will join him, so the whole place will be like a chaotic circus. Mum will fuss over me like I'm still five years old and my sister, Mae, told me neither she nor Dylan, my other brother, are coming. Mae's going to her fiancé's parents and Dylan will be somewhere out on the coral reef, fishing. It's one of those occasions I dread—and I hope that Dad doesn't push me over the edge one day and start a physical fight.'

'Oh.' Francene stared at him in horror. 'Really? Things are that bad?'

'Yes. When we were young, he was pretty generous with his fists. But back then, I was so frightened of him I used to hide until he settled down. That's why I left home as soon as I finished studying—and used my savings from all the years of rearing calves and cleaning out the manure from under the woolshed to head to the UK—as far away from him as I could get. At least we had opportunities to earn money from our farm chores, and Mum made sure we were paid for the work we did. She did the books so Dad couldn't argue.'

'Don't blame you,' Francene said, studying him with a worried frown. 'How do you think you'll get on now? Will you be safe?'

He grunted. 'Yeah. I haven't seen him for years. Even after my accident, it was only Mum who visited. But Mae assures me he's mellowed with age. Still—it's not exactly the Christmas I'm looking forward to.' He shot her a rueful smile. 'Anyway, let's move on to more exciting things, like moving your furniture and putting the boxes into the right rooms so you can unpack.'

'Sounds great. Then you should stay for dinner. I haven't cooked for myself while I've been at the hotel. But now I've got my own place again, I'm looking forward to concocting some of my favourites. Tonight it's marinated chicken and stir-fried vegetables.'

'Yum. Sounds delicious.'

His smile widened as their eyes met, and it was all he could do to concentrate on the job at hand.

It was after nine before they strolled outside and stood beside Bryn's ute, a sudden awkwardness causing them a few moments of silence.

'What have you got planned tomorrow?' Francene eventually asked.

Uncertain whether her question was simply out of politeness or whether it suggested she might invite him to join her again, he hesitated before answering. 'Oh, just the usual—tidy up the shed first, I reckon.' He shared a wry grin. 'I've made my parents a garden seat but it's not quite finished. The timber needs one more coat of stain then the final seal. After that, I guess I'll load it onto the ute and start getting ready to head to Armidale on Christmas Eve.'

'Sounds beautiful. Don't forget to take a photo. I'd love to see it.'

Joy surged in him again. 'What are your plans for tomorrow?'

She cast an arm toward the cottage. 'Continue unpacking I guess.'

'Why don't you pop up to my place for a pot of tea when you're ready for a break? I'll show you what I've been making, and we can sit on the veranda and enjoy the scenery,' he finished with a cheeky grin that, in the dark, he hoped she didn't take the wrong way.

'Sounds lovely,' she breathed, all hint of uncertainty erased.

He stepped closer and gave her a quick kiss on the cheek, his pulse thumping in his chest. 'Thanks for the lovely dinner.'

She raised a hand and touched his arm lightly. 'Thanks for your help.'

He ducked his head and opened the car door, sliding into the seat before the urge to take her in his arms and hold her in a crushing hug became a reality. *Too soon. You'll see her tomorrow*

Then, with a wave, he reversed onto the road, cast a last glance toward her, and drove away. As the lights faded behind him and the quiet of the night seeped into his soul, he whooped loudly then laughed.

What the hell is happening to me? I feel like one life has gone and another is just beginning—a much more exciting one.

33

———

Francene woke early, filled with an energy she hadn't experienced for a long time. She'd lain awake, reflecting on Bryn's visit long after he'd gone home, wondering what had happened to her resolve to have nothing more to do with men. Relieved that he'd been so kind and considerate, not leaping in with praises and flattery like Kyle had, their conversation had been friendly, giving her the chance to observe him without feeling any pressure. It had made her relax and enjoy his company without one hint of threat.

She'd briefly puzzled over what she had seen in Kyle. Obviously his smooth talking and constant attention had swept her off her feet. But now, she could see how naïve she'd been, and her insides squirmed at the memories.

Eventually, dismissing her deceased husband with a grunt, she'd switched her thoughts to Eleanor, wondering if she had returned to the hotel or was staying another night at the farm. She'd sent a silent thanks to her for introducing her to Featherwood Falls, then fallen into a dreamless sleep.

After a morning walk and breakfast on her back porch overlooking the bush, she remembered the explanation of religieuse she'd given Bryn. She would make some this morning and take them with her when she visited that afternoon.

With her decision made, she plugged her phone in and tapped her music app before singing along as she unpacked boxes.

Hours later, with a cooling rack filled with the delicious little pastries, her bedroom and kitchen fully organised, and a load of washing on the line, she jumped into the shower and dressed in a pair of shorts and her favourite pink shirt.

Familiar now with the minor country roads and the need to drive slowly in the loose gravel, she made her way up the rise from the valley and pulled into Bryn's backyard.

He greeted her from the open work shed with a wide grin, propping a straw broom against the wall.

After carefully manoeuvring the container of pastries out of the back seat, she handed them to him. 'I come bearing gifts.'

He laughed. 'Thank you. Time for a cuppa then?'

'Sounds lovely.'

She followed him inside, surprised at the tidy kitchen with the dishcloth folded over the centre of the double sink and not a sign of dirty dishes. Trying not to compare his obvious habits with those of Kyle's, she placed the container on the counter, waiting while he filled the electric jug and plugged it in.

'Herbal? English breakfast or rooibos?'

'Do you have peppermint?'

'Of course.' He opened a drawer with a flourish, displaying a row of different tea packets.

They sat on the front veranda looking across the lower edges of Featherwood Station and down to where roofs and chimneys of houses in town were visible above the row of trees. The bench underneath her was plain but comfortable, the tray containing a teapot, two mugs, and a plate filled with Francene's pastries resting on a little table with exquisitely carved legs.

She pointed to them admiringly. 'How gorgeous.'

'My first attempt,' he said, angling his head as though embarrassed to admit it.

She gasped. 'Really?' Pressing a hand on her mouth for a moment, she narrowed her eyes at him. 'Would you be able to make some furniture for my business? I'll pay you, of course—and there's no hurry.' She gabbled out the words, her voice high with admiration.

'Of course.' He grinned. I've got a few orders, but I'll find time to make whatever you'd like.'

'I can't wait to see what's in the shed.'

Their eyes met for a second as he poured the tea. 'And I can't wait to taste these delicious little—what do you call them again? Religious-something-or-others.'

'Religieuse,' she laughed, 'but you can call them whatever you like.'

He picked one up, inspected it, and took a large bite. Savouring it, he closed his eyes before swallowing. 'I'll stick to calling them little nun pastries,' he said, while making blissful, appreciative murmurs as he ate. 'Doubt I'll be on any cooking shows in the near future, so I'm sure no one will mind.' He promptly leaned forward and helped himself to another.

They sat there talking and laughing about nothing and everything, the atmosphere relaxed and peaceful as Bryn topped up their tea and they each ate more religieuse.

Over an hour passed in what seemed a flash to Francene before Bryn picked up the tray and inclined his head toward the door.

'Ready for a tour of the shed?' he asked.

Francene stood. 'Sure.'

Uncertain of what she'd expected, Francene's eyes widened. A row of tools lay on the bench in a neat row, and along the middle of the wide floor was a stand holding what looked to her like lethal pieces of electrical equipment.

'I've bought a few bits and pieces over the last couple of weeks and they're certainly making life easier,' Bryn said, pointing to a complicated contraption fixed to a small table. 'That's the lathe I picked up second hand from a guy in Stanthorpe. He hadn't used it in years apparently but kept it in good nick.'

Francene studied it more closely, nodding with agreement. 'What's it used for?'

'Turning wood like the legs of the table you admired. I'll be able to make use of it for other decorative items instead of hand-carving them.'

'Oh.' Her gaze moved to a beautiful two-person wooden couch, its solid, curved seat carved from a single slab of timber and the slatted back inset with an oval pattern depicting trees and two tiny birds. She bent down to look more closely at the centrepiece. 'This is gorgeous. Is it the one you made for your parents?'

'Yeah. I found a fallen trunk up the back of Featherwood Station. Ginny and Kirk said I could have it, but I couldn't move it.' He laughed. 'I was still trying to figure out how to get it here when Kirk arrived at the shed with it on the back of their truck. Because it wasn't very long, he'd picked it up with the front-end loader. We struck a deal—he'd take it to the sawmill and have it cut into slabs if I turned one of them into a two-seater for them.'

'So have you already made theirs?'

He shook his head. 'No. They said they're in no hurry, so I made this one first. Then I'll get on to the others after Christmas.' Unable to keep the pride from his voice, he straightened, an excited grin on his face. 'Got an order from Frank and Lola, and Emma and Ryan too—and now you.'

'Fantastic.' Her admiration for this man soared in a hot wave. Not once had he mentioned his physical restrictions, nor had he expected help from anyone else. She studied the height of his ute and frowned. 'So how are you going to get it into the back of your ute to take to your parents' place? Would you like me to help you?'

'No way. It's really heavy. I've asked Rhys for a hand in the morning.'

A loud moo distracted them, and Francene looked up in surprise. 'A friend?'

He laughed. 'That's Buttons. She's one of the Shepherd family's hand-reared calves—now a rather large and noisy cow. She comes to the fence every evening for a pat and a handful of hay. It's really the hay she comes for.'

'Can I feed her?' Francene beamed with delight,

transported back to her teenage years on Marianne's grandparents' farm.

'Sure.' He pointed to a bale of lucerne hay on the shed floor behind his ute.

They walked over to it, and he separated half a biscuit of the fragrant green legume before handing it to her.

'Just make sure your hand is well back. She won't bite, but cows have a long, very rough tongue and that can startle you a bit.'

She followed his instructions, meeting his encouraging smile as she reached out to the huge cow.

The sun had lowered in the sky and a cool breeze brushed away the searing heat of earlier. A family of magpies sat on the shed roof, their heads lifted as they warbled.

'Gosh it's lovely here, isn't it? You must be really enjoying it?'

He nodded. 'Sure am.' He glanced at his watch. 'There's still an hour or so of daylight. Would you like to come for a walk with me up to the falls?'

Her forehead creased. The only falls she'd seen since arriving in the town were those near the waterhole where she had sat and read while staying at the hotel. They weren't big—more of a cascade really. But either way, she couldn't see how they could walk from here and return before dark.

As if sensing her confusion, he pointed up the hill

above them. 'You're probably thinking about the town falls. These are much more spectacular. They're on Featherwood Station, but Ginny and Kirk have given me permission to walk up there any time I like.'

'Okay then. She looked down at her sneakers. 'Will my shoes be alright, or do I need something more sturdy?'

He reached out a hand. 'You'll be fine.'

She took it, revelling in the firm, reassuring grip that encompassed hers, and her heart sang.

THEY SET off at a steady pace, holding hands the whole way. Surprised that Bryn's limp seemed to have almost disappeared, Francene had to walk briskly to keep up with him, realising she wasn't as fit as she thought she was.

When the sound of water reached them and the cool, tree-filled valley encompassed their hot, tired bodies, she breathed a sigh of pure bliss.

They sat beside the pool, bare feet dangling in the water as the sun drooped in the sky behind them, soaking in the atmosphere while birds twitted around them, unafraid.

Bryn squeezed her hand. 'It'll be dark soon. Time to go.'

She nodded, reluctantly sliding her feet back into

her shoes before she stood up. 'Thank you for bringing me here. It's been the best day ever—and I reckon it'll be the best Christmas, too.'

He smiled at her, but she glimpsed the fleeting doubt in his eyes.

Remembering his bitterness when discussing his family, she wished she hadn't mentioned Christmas. In the morning he would travel to his childhood home.

She rested her hand on his arm. 'I've got a good feeling about this—and luckily, I've got better at listening to my instincts. Things won't be as bad in Armidale as you're expecting and I'll be here, looking forward to your return.'

He held her for a few seconds, and she clung to him, hoping the day would come soon—the day when she could shed the last of her resentment against Kyle and let her emotions run free.

Ginny stood with her hands on her hips, biting her bottom lip as she studied the pine from all angles. Decorating the Christmas tree had always been a combined effort when the girls were growing up, but over the past few years, it had been left to her. Mostly she ensured it was in place and decorated well before Christmas, but this year she had barely given it consideration.

Kirk ambled into the room and slumped on the couch. 'Looks nice,' he said.

Ginny tilted her head. 'I haven't got the angel on top right. She's lopsided.'

Chuckling, he got to his feet and straightened the delicate ornament, ensuring he secured her feet to the topmost point. 'Happy now?'

'Yes. Thank you.' She sighed. 'Tomorrow is

Christmas Eve, Briony and the troops will be home, and I've hardly done a thing.'

'You've made cookies.' He moved to the bench and picked up a peanut brownie before chomping into it with obvious delight. 'Didn't you say everyone's bringing food and Alex and Sam have got drinks all sorted? What else do we need to do?'

'Are you serious?' Ginny answered crossly, her skin clammy from yet another hot flush and her cheeks burning with frustration. 'For a start, there are a hundred sodden bales of hay in the paddock that need moving off the fresh lucerne before they kill the living plants underneath them. Then there's the Christmas lamb that's supposed to be hanging in the meat-house but is still running around the paddock—and the peas that should have been picked days ago and frozen. They're probably bursting out of their shrivelled shells by now.'

He popped the last bite of cookie into his mouth and pressed his palms lightly on either side of her face. 'It's going to be okay. I've talked to Claire, and she and Rhys are shifting the hay as soon as Rhys finishes work today. I told them to pile it up behind the garden shed, and after Christmas, you and I can split the bales open and used the rotting hay to mulch the garden and around the trees. At least it's not a total waste.'

She cursed silently, reluctant to be pacified. 'And what about the meat? Lola's bringing chickens and

Ryan and Emma have organised seafood, but you're not in a fit state to kill a lamb—and even if you were, we haven't got enough time for it to hang before Christmas day.' The desperation that had been brewing inside her during Kirk's hospitalisation had continued since arriving home, and now it threatened to explode.

'So, we'll have beef,' he said calmly. 'There's plenty of it in the freezer and if we sort through, I'm sure we'll find a couple of excellent pieces of rump we can slow roast. I'll do that now.'

Her lip quivered and she turned away. 'Fine. I'm going to feed the dogs and lock up the chooks.' Then she snatched the scrap bucket from the kitchen bench and stomped outside.

By the time she'd emptied the scraps, counted the chooks, and locked the gate, the heat had left her face and she followed the doctor's advice, taking several deep, slow breaths while she focused on the positives in her life. She reached the kennels, her steps measured and her mind finally clearing. What did it matter if they ate beef instead of lamb? And if the peas were past eating, she'd use frozen. As for the hay, it had already caused enough problems, so she relented and switched her mind away from it.

As she leaned against the fence post watching the dogs running around, stretching their legs and toileting away from the kennels, a whinny sounded from across the paddock behind her. She turned, her face softening as she focused on the ancient chestnut pony hobbling toward her.

'Hello, old man.' She rubbed Rusty's nose and leaned her forehead against his. 'Are you lonely? Wanted to have a chat, eh? I know how you feel.'

Lifting her gaze to the paddock beyond, her eyes misted as she thought about Flash, the gentle chestnut pony they'd had since Briony was little. When Claire had come along, both girls had shared him, but by the time Claire was five, she'd demanded her own pony and so they had bought Rusty. Both ponies were so similar, the girls had won many "pairs" classes at pony club gymkhanas and shows. Then, as they'd grown, Akela, the lovely bay mare they all enjoyed riding had come along. Splash, the Appaloosa Claire and Rhys liked the most, had been next, and then the following year Claire had purchased Tango, the smart, brown pony she used as a learner's mount for her riding students.

Ginny stared into Rusty's clouded eyes, stroking him and talking quietly as his ears flicked back and forth. 'You miss your special mate, don't you?' It had been sudden. One day Flash was standing at the stable gate, nickering for his "gummy nuts" and the next, when he didn't show up, they'd found him curled up like a dog under his favourite tree, dead. She and the girls had shed buckets of tears while Kirk got out the front-end loader and dug an enormous grave as close to the tree as he could get. Even now, months later, Ginny could see the slight mound marked by a white wooden cross at the bottom of the paddock.

'Come on then. Let's get you a treat before the others spot us.' She opened the shed door and scooped pony pellets from a drum before dropping them into the feed bin attached to the fence.

Fifteen minutes later, she returned to the homestead as a cooling breeze ruffled her hair. She lifted her chin to the fading sun and allowed the final threads of despondency to float away.

35

———————

*A*s Bryn swung the ute onto the highway south, his stomach clenched. He lowered the travel cup into the holder and sighed. Coffee wasn't the right soother for apprehension. Perhaps he should have made himself a camomile tea, or better still, added a slug of whisky.

It had been a long time since his previous trip to Armidale and despite his reluctance, a frisson of pleasure rose in his chest. The countryside had never looked better—the heavy rain from days earlier had washed away the dust and boosted the grass from a sunburnt brown to a fresh, bright green. Even the sheep seemed cleaner than he remembered, the hills more inviting. *Maybe one day I'll return.* Then a flashback of his father's anger resurged and a bitter taste formed in his mouth. *Not while you're alive.*

He drove slowly up the curved driveway, silently admiring the glossy, rust-coloured cattle in the front paddock—his father's pride and joy. On either side of the gravel drive, the brilliant blue of his mother's hydrangeas and agapanthus drew him toward the central garden filled with red and white roses, their colours contrasting perfectly.

A low-set stone homestead came into view, and a pang of nostalgia touched Bryn. Although it held traumatic memories for him, it had been home for seventeen years. Happy times had occurred as well as sad, and he sucked in a breath, determined to focus on them. He was no longer that skinny teenager trying hard to copy his brothers but never quite achieving his father's expectations. He swallowed the tight lump in his throat as a part of him ached to heal the family rift.

His eyebrows raised as he caught sight of a shiny new shed and silo next to the original grey corrugated iron one. He couldn't recall his mother mentioning its construction, but he felt no disappointment. *Probably built when I was in hospital and was only registering half of what I was told.*

He parked in the shade of the ancient plane tree to the side of the house—the one he and Mae had spent hours in, building cubbyhouses, reading, and taking turns sitting astride the less sturdy branches and rocking them just enough to pretend they were on a bucking bronc but not enough to cause the branch to break.

The screen door slammed, and his mother hurried toward him, drying her hands on a tea towel before slinging it over her shoulder and holding out her arms.

'Welcome home!' The glee in her voice softened his face as they hugged.

While she fussed over him, running one question after another—'How is the pain? Do you need to rest? How was the drive? Much traffic about?'

'I'm fine, Mum,' was all he could say before a tall, thickset man emerged from the house and ambled toward him, his balding head bare in the sunlight and his hands shaking.

Bryn froze. *Dad?* Not the strong, belligerent person he had visited years earlier. This was an elderly man, familiar, but one who appeared to either have a medical condition or was very nervous.

He met his mother's eyes, and she gave a tiny shake of her head as if to say, *'Don't ask.'*

Plastering a smile on his face, he reached out a hand and grasped his father's tremulous paw. 'Gidday, Dad. Merry Christmas.'

The old man cleared his throat. 'Yes, well. Same to you,' he croaked.

To hide his shock, Bryn turned back to the ute and dragged out his bag.

'Your old room is just the same, Bryn. Waiting for you,' his mother said.

They walked slowly toward the kitchen door, his mother leading with her arm tucked into his father's as Bryn followed.

'Cattle look good,' Bryn said as they removed their boots on the porch.

His father lifted his gaze, the faded blue eyes brightening. 'Been a good season.' Then he stumbled through the open door, bumping his shoulder on the frame before slumping into a kitchen chair.

Trying to resist staring at the shaking hands, Bryn faked a cheerful grin. 'And how was the harvest?'

The response was as Bryn expected. Provided the conversation was all about farming, his father was alert and interested. It was when politics, education, or the state of the roads were mentioned that his voice became louder and his temper flared. Although this time Bryn was surprised to notice subtle changes in his father that someone outside the family may not—things like staring into space at regular intervals and gazing around the room as if to familiarise himself with somewhere new.

Over the lunch table, the old man sipped his tea noisily, holding the mug with both hands and slopping it on the tablecloth when he put it down. There was no apology—almost as if he hadn't noticed, but Bryn's mother flicked a worried look at Bryn each time, pandering to her husband with brittle, poorly disguised actions.

It was late that night, well after the old man had retired to bed, that Bryn and his mother sat on the front veranda enjoying a glass of wine.

'I'm sorry I didn't tell you. We only got the diagnosis ourselves last week, although he has been failing for a while.'

'Parkinson's disease?'

She nodded. 'Yes. Initially they thought it might be multiple sclerosis, but tests revealed Parkinson's. Not sure which is worse, but it certainly has changed him. He won't show it, but he's frightened. You know how he's always been in control. Now he's losing that and he doesn't know how to cope.'

A wave of sympathy flashed through Bryn, surprising him. *Perhaps it's because I know what it feels like to be helpless and have to rely on others.* It was just a shame that it took something like this to bring about enough changes in his father's personality to feel sorry for him.

'What's the prognosis?'

'I wish I had a crystal ball. But I don't and neither do the doctors. He's on medication but it's taken so long for him to accept he's not the man he used to be, it's too late for any of those early interventions.' She heaved a sigh. 'I guess we'll just take each day as it comes and see what happens.'

'Does Mae know?'

'Yes. I only told her yesterday though. Didn't want her upset until we had a confirmed diagnosis. Owen knows, of course. He's been slowly taking over much of the workload, although your father still likes to make the decisions.' They shared a rueful smile as she continued. 'I'm thankful that I still maintain the farm accounts though. Sandra wanted to take them over when the boys started school, but I told her I'm not dead yet and when I feel I am no longer coping, we'll discuss the matter then.'

Bryn chuckled. Sandra was Owen's wife—a strong, controlling woman, not unlike her husband. He'd only met her a few times but sometimes wondered what went on behind their closed doors and who won their battles. Or perhaps they didn't have many. Maybe that's the secret—did a successful marriage require both partners to have the same personalities? He glanced across at his mother. Although it had always been his father who ranted and roared, throwing his weight and his temper around, it had been his mother who, with a core of steel, had made the final decisions and supported her four children with theirs.

Bryn yawned. It had been a long day and he would need all the energy he had to get through Christmas. 'I'm off to bed, Mum. See you in the morning.'

'Good night, love. Sleep well.'

He could feel her gaze following him down the hallway and he turned back to smile.

Maybe tomorrow I'll tell her about Francene.

36

———

Christmas Day dawned still and hot, the early morning temperature and yet another hot flush chasing Ginny out of bed and on to the veranda.

After the previous two days stressing unnecessarily, everything seemed to be falling in to place. Lola had rung confirming she had made a trifle and had three chickens roasting in the oven. She also added that Emma had collected the prawns from the fish man outside the hotel.

A gentle piece of music began its notes, filtering to her from the kitchen. *My phone? Who rings at five-thirty in the morning?*

'Hello?'

'Hi, Ginny. It's Sophie. Sorry to call so early but I knew you'd probably be up already.'

Tempted to deliver an eye roll at Sophie's statement, she frowned instead. 'Is everything alright?'

'Oh yes. Everything's fine. As you know, the others got home later than expected, so Alex and Briony didn't get time to make the dishes they said they would. So I'm in the kitchen now with Eleanor. We thought we'd give them a good start to Christmas by making something. Could you give us some suggestions please?'

Ginny smiled at the vision of an octogenarian and a one-handed young woman attempting to cook Christmas goodies in an unfamiliar kitchen—although, perhaps after the previous week with Briony, Alex, and his parents away, they were a little more familiar than previously.

'How about I come down and give you a hand? Kirk's organised everything here and can feed up while the meat's cooking. See you in half an hour.'

The audible sigh from Sophie was tangible, and she grinned. It seemed that three cooks in the Cunningham family were enough.

She showered and dressed, tying her hair back in a ponytail before planting a kiss on Kirk's drowsy cheek. 'See you in an hour or two,' she whispered. 'Don't forget to give Rusty an extra scoop of gummy-nuts.'

Responding with a drowsy grunt, he sat up and rubbed his face as she gave him a wave and fled outside.

An hour later, a large potato bake sat on the stove waiting to be cooked and, despite her plastered wrist, Sophie had assembled the ingredients for two salads. One would be a Moroccan rice and nut version she had watched Alex make on a regular basis, and the other a leafy platter laden with colourful raw vegetables and with a fresh citrus dressing.

Briony appeared in the doorway, rubbing her startled eyes as if a family of elves had taken over her kitchen. 'What's going on here?'

'We thought we'd let you and Alex have a sleep in.' Sophie grinned.

Briony snorted a half-hearted laugh before moving to the coffee machine. 'Nice thought. Thanks. You must be ready for coffee then?'

Breakfast was followed by more coffee and within the estimated two hours, Ginny headed home with Sophie sitting beside her.

'I might not take after my parents or brother in the kitchen, but I can decorate a pretty awesome Christmas table.'

They exchanged smiles as they drove past Francene's cottage. 'Isn't it wonderful what she's planning?' Sophie said.

'Yes. She seems to have settled into our community well—and I admit I'm looking forward to tasting some of those lovely pastries she makes and sitting on that cute veranda drinking pots of tea.'

'Ooh, yum. Me too,' Sophie added. 'It's lovely having another younger couple move into the town. Kind of balances out the number of older folk living here.'

Ginny spluttered with laughter. 'And I suppose Kirk and I are in the "older folk" category?'

Sophie blushed pink, shaking her head wildly. 'Oh no, that's not what I meant. It's just nice to have more …' she paused for a second as if unable to find the right word, 'of my age group,' she finished.

Ginny nodded. 'I agree—and I think you might be right. About the couple, I mean. Francene and Bryn may have arrived here separately, but I think there could be romance in the air.'

'I reckon this town has something in the water—look how many couples have met and married here or are about to—you and Kirk for a start.'

Ginny smiled softly. 'Perhaps you're right. Are you suggesting there's wedding bells afoot for you and Sam?'

Sophie blushed again. 'No. At least not yet. I was thinking about Ashleigh and Damian—their wedding is New Year's Eve and now there's Francene and Bryn.'

'Let's not get too hasty. They've only known each other for a few weeks.'

Sophie hugged her knees to her with a smug look on her face. 'Well, I'm willing to bet that within a year, those two will be married.'

Ginny laughed, pulling into the shed and switching off the engine. 'Come on then, Cupid. We've got a table to set for …' she paused, her fingers flicking as she ran through the names in her head, 'nineteen adults and one baby.'

GINNY CAST her eyes around the group sitting along either side of the trestle tables that extended from one end of the veranda to the other. From Eleanor to little Liam, she was surrounded by those she loved most— her own daughters and sons-in-law, Alex's parents, her sister-in-law, Sarah, and nephew, Andrew, best friends forever, Lola and Frank, and their son, Ryan, daughter-in-law, Emma, and granddaughter, Zoe. Then, sitting at the head of the table was her beloved Kirk, and beside him, Francene, the gentle young woman who Eleanor had befriended and brought into their community, and beside her, Sophie and Sam, the caring and delightful New Zealand man who had breezed into Featherwood Falls Hotel months earlier.

She blew out a happy sigh, pushing the never-ending worry about Glenrowan and its troubled owner to the back of her mind.

While the valley baked under the summer sun, the feast set out on the dining table in buffet style gradually disappeared—the main course followed by a range of desserts, thanks to Lola, Francene, and Sarah, who had arrived bearing a cheesecake big enough to feed a shearing gang.

While some, like Ryan, Emma, Liam and Eleanor, Aileen and Bruce, drifted home for an afternoon nap before re-joining the party on dusk, the others stayed until after dark, sharing stories, taking a stroll to the falls, and eating the leftovers from lunch.

When the day was over, Ginny fell into bed, relieved everyone had enjoyed their day. As the first gentle snores emanated from her husband, Ginny turned onto her side and stared through the window at the moon, its pale glow illuminating the flowers and the shadows of trees.

A movement in the garden spiked a sudden stab of terror through her, the previous exhaustion dissipating in an instant.

After creeping to the French doors, she pressed her face against the glass and held her breath, releasing it slowly as Kimba, one of her tabby cats, mooched across the lawn.

Was that all it was? She shook her head. *I've eaten too much and am imagining things.*

But deep in her gut, something niggled—and the hairs on her arms stood to attention.

37

The drive back to Featherwood Falls bore no comparison to his trip home. Still reeling from his father's farewell as the ute progressively reduced the kilometres, Bryn reflected on the previous day.

Unlike any other Christmas he had spent with his family, this time, there had been no disagreements—unless the tussle between Owen and Sandra's boys, now aged eight and ten, over a computer game counted. Owen had shown the only hint of interest and compassion for his younger brother Bryn ever remembered. He'd asked in an attentive, genuine manner about Bryn's new-found hobby-come-business and frowned with concern as they discussed Bryn's injuries and recovery program. Sandra, too, had been less domineering than he remembered, her perfect makeup barely hiding the dark lines under her eyes, and she'd helped prepare and serve the meal without telling his mother what to do.

But the highlight of the day had been when he'd uncovered the seat and asked Owen to help him lift it off the ute. Tears had sprung to his mother's eyes and when his father sat on it beside her, he had gazed at Bryn with respectful awe. The swirl of warm delight still fluttered in his stomach. Then, when saying goodbye that morning, his father had squeezed his hand between his two shaking palms, and Bryn had stared straight into the blue eyes that had once terrified him and were now pale and watery.

'Thanks for coming, son. It's been a real good Christmas.'

It had been the first time Bryn could remember being thanked by his father for anything—and his heart had soared.

It was after eight before Francene woke, by which time the birds were making a racket in the tree outside her window and the iron roof crackled as the heat built up.

Reliving the previous day, she stretched and smiled to herself. It had been wonderful. Encompassed by the group of friendly, casual people, she had experienced a welcome unlike any she'd had since before her grandparents died. *Maybe the box of eclairs helped?* The skills and technique Henry had taught her had never faded, but it had taken Eleanor's initial encouragement to set her on the path she'd dreamed of. Now, here she was, waking up in her own bed in her own house—in a town she was coming to love and with a warmth in her belly after the effusive compliments everyone had paid her after eating her pastries.

'Can't wait until you open your tearoom,' Ryan had said.

With a quizzical stare from his mother, he had quickly added, 'Especially as it will take some of the pressure off Mum to bake lamingtons all the time.'

Everyone had laughed, including Lola, who simply said she was happy to hand over the town's cooking crown and enjoy spending time with her grandchildren, Liam and Zoe.

'And I'm relieved that I will no longer have to dream up new ideas for afternoon teas,' Briony said. 'While Alex and I learned heaps during our chef training, when we bought this hotel, the plan was to serve three meals a day—which was two more than Ned ever did.' She smiled at Lola. 'We supported each other and it's been great, but it will be even more wonderful to send visitors to "Tea, Tarts and Treasures" for a light lunch or afternoon tea and invite them to join us at the hotel for dinner at night.'

Lola nodded, her flashing Christmas earrings distracting a tired Liam who, sitting on her knee, reached up to one and tried to stuff it in his mouth.

Francene had restricted her glasses of wine to two and had sipped them slowly as she observed the interaction between the guests, especially Andrew and Zoe —a couple who, despite their obvious age gap, appeared to have a comfortable, caring relationship she could only dream of.

Guessing Andrew to be around his late twenties, she remembered Lola mentioning Zoe had only one more year of school before she planned to head to university to study veterinary science. While reflecting on her own goals, her mind kept flicking to Bryn and wondering how he was getting on with his family. A steely determination settled inside her. No matter what, hard work and true grit would ensure the success of "Tea, Tarts and Treasures". If her relationship with Bryn was meant to be, then she certainly would let it— without repeating the mistakes she'd made in the past.

Her phone rang and she snatched it up, hoping it might be Bryn. It wasn't.

'Hello, darling,' her mother said in her familiar French accent. 'Merry Christmas.' Her mum sprang to life as she clicked the correct icon and they beamed at each other.

'Hey, Mama. Same to you.' Although they didn't

speak very often, the familiar sound of her mother's voice and the well-known face—recognisably similar to her own but with less vibrant blue eyes and dark hair now streaked with grey—sent a twinge of homesickness through her. Francene's chest tightened as past enjoyable family Christmases flooded back. 'Is Dad there?'

'Yes, of course.' The handsome, creased face of her father pressed against her mother's as they shared the past few weeks of events in both France and Featherwood Falls.

Her mother had flown over following Kyle's death but had stayed only days, voicing her long-held opinion of her son-in-law that Francene had been shocked to hear. She had shared none of the negative side of their marriage with her family, eventually believing his repeated insistence that his gambling and "getting upset with her" was her fault and not his. But after his funeral, her mother had held her in a long hug and whispered the words, 'I never trusted him, and I'm pleased he's gone. Now you're free.' Francene had been shocked.

Except for a quick call the day Francene signed the contract for her house, they had not spoken since before Francene had moved out of the Brisbane home. Now she could elaborate on all that had happened, including meeting Bryn.

Half an hour later, they blew kisses to each other via the video link and ended the call.

Strengthened by thoughts of happy family times, she leapt out of bed and dressed in shorts and a long-sleeved cotton shirt. While she waited for the council licence, she would dig over the gardens and replant. After all, what was a cottage without a pretty garden?

THE PREVIOUS EVENING'S unease had ensured a restless night for Ginny and although still tired, she dragged herself out of bed at six o'clock, dressed, and headed out to feed the animals. The heat played havoc with her hormones, and as she leaned against the post outside the dog kennels, the lure of the falls beckoned.

'Come on, dogs. Let's go for a swim.'

Shedding her clothes and dropping them far enough away from the edge for the wet, excitable kelpies not to shake themselves on them, she trod carefully to the water's edge and lowered herself in.

The heavy rain had washed the edges clean and flushed debris down the creek, leaving the pond sparkling and fresh.

As she wallowed, all but Drum leapt in and out, swimming after each other in circles and bringing a smile to her face.

She waded to where Drum sat on the flat, granite

edge and gathered him in her arms. 'It's okay, mate. I won't let you go. Come on.'

Reluctantly, the little dog allowed her to drag him into the water, where he paddled frantically while she kept a firm grip on his collar. After one circuit of the pool, she returned him to firm footing and followed him.

Minutes later, cool and refreshed, and with the team of kelpies trotting along behind her in a subdued fashion, they headed home. As she reached the crest of the hill, she breathed a sigh of contentment. Her beloved old ewes grazed around the chook pen and her thoughts flicked to the sale of the rest of her stud sheep. Unwilling to leave Kirk after his hospitalisation, her agent had arranged for them to be collected by a stock carrier and when, that evening, he had phoned her with the sale report, she had been filled with delight. It had been one of the best she had ever received.

Maybe with Kirk's latest find from the mine, and my sheep money, we can give some serious thought to our first ever overseas holiday.

They reached the kennels and all but Drum jumped into their pens, waiting patiently for Ginny to shut their gates. When she turned to call him to her, her jaw dropped. A low growl sounded from the dog's throat and his hackles stood in a spiky row along his backbone.

She followed his gaze to the car—a small dark blue version of a four-wheel drive more suited to a city than to Featherwood Falls. It parked in front of the picket gate leading to the house and a man climbed out of the passenger seat, his face lifted to hers.

'Nigel?' she whispered. Ice ran through her veins.

38

———

With her heart racing and her breath coming in short, rapid pants, she glanced around, searching for Kirk. Cursing silently at herself for leaving her phone on the kitchen bench, she ignored the pounding roar in her ears, reasoning he was most likely on the veranda cleaning the barbeque after roasting yesterday's beef. At least she hoped so—and that he, too, had seen Nigel.

While nervous fury bubbled and built inside her, she ordered Drum into his pen and latched the gate. 'It'll be alright, little man. We've got this.'

Then she marched toward the car, taking slow, measured breaths, hoping by the time she reached Nigel, she showed none of the initial fear that had slammed her like the sudden closing of a door.

'Hello, Nigel.' She looked the small man up and down, relieved he appeared as nervous as she was.

'Ginny. Have you got a few minutes to talk?'

A second man remained in the driver's seat, his clean-shaven face partially disguised by sunglasses and a cap.

'I guess so. Okay if we stay out here? I have visitors and ...' she lied, glancing at her watch, 'it is only eight-thirty on Boxing Day. Does Andrew know you're here?' She hoped so, despite there being no suggestion of Nigel's release the previous day. The shock was enough for her, but if Andrew was not prepared for Nigel's arrival home, she wasn't sure how he would react.

'Not yet. I'm sorry I'm invading your privacy so early on a public holiday, but I hope what I have to tell you will excuse my rudeness.'

Taken aback by the man's politeness, she rocked slightly and uncurled her clenched fists. 'Go on.'

He looked at the ground and then back at her, their eyes level and his twitching with obvious unease. 'First, I want to apologise ... for everything that happened. I never meant to hurt Lyndon, and I have regretted my actions every day since then.'

She gave a slight nod but said nothing.

He turned toward the car with the hint of a smile on his face. 'I have met someone very special, and I will never live on Glenrowan again.'

She nearly fell over as he delivered this news,

closing her spontaneously opened mouth with a snap and narrowing her eyes as the comment sank in.

'Okay,' she said slowly, hoping he would elaborate without prompting.

'I am moving to Tasmania and will sell the property. I thought you might like to have first refusal—by way of an apology.'

'Really?' Ginny couldn't contain herself, a flood of relief overwhelming her as Kirk opened the gate and joined them.

For a few moments, no one said anything. Then Ginny lifted her chin and turned to Kirk. 'Nigel has decided to sell Glenrowan and has given me first refusal.'

A nerve twitched on Kirk's cheek, probably barely discernible to those who didn't know him well. But Ginny did, and her confidence grew, acknowledging the sign as an attempt to control his emotions.

'Thank you, Nigel. Of course we'll need to think about your offer and discuss it with the family. When do you need our answer?' she said.

He shrugged. 'As soon as possible, I guess. We're staying in Warwick until I can get this sorted out, then we'll drive south.'

'Very well. Do you have a price in mind? Or will you take offers?'

He shook his head. 'I'm not sure of values, but my lawyer will help with any questions you may have.

These are the firm's business details and I've written my number on the back.'

She nodded briskly, taking the card he handed her. 'Thank you. I'll be in touch.'

His solemn face moved slightly in what may have been an attempt at a smile, then he turned and walked back to the vehicle.

She reached for Kirk's hand as the car drove away. 'I don't believe it!' Her eyes met Kirk's wide-eyed stare. 'I'd better ring Andrew immediately—before they shock him too.'

They turned, and Ginny ran with Kirk striding behind.

'GIDDAY, AUNTIE GINNY. EVERYTHING OKAY?' Andrew said with a yawn.

'Very much so.' Her voice rose as she spoke quickly and tapped the speaker icon so Kirk could hear the conversation. 'Nigel's just been here and he's on his way to see you. He wants to sell Glenrowan and has given me first offer.'

'Far out! Are you kidding?' For an instant, neither of them said a word.

'I know. It's an enormous shock. After three genera-tions, I never for a moment thought the Shepherd family had a hope of regaining that chunk of land. It's almost like history has turned full circle—that is, if we can afford to buy it.'

He emitted a wild, excited laugh. 'Do you remember when you told me how worried you were about Nigel's release from prison? I mentioned Mum and I had a plan.' He continued without waiting for her to answer. 'Well, that plan was to offer him such a good price for this place, he wouldn't think about refusing.'

'Really?'

'Yes, really.' He paused. 'Hey, they're coming up the drive now. Don't worry. Whatever he says, this farm will be back in the Shepherd family within weeks—without my father having any part of it or financial connection to it. If you decide not to make an offer, we'll work it out between us and I'll buy it. Gotta go. They're getting out of the car.'

'Great. Talk soon.'

Ginny slumped in the chair, her hand still clasping the phone and with an incredulous grin on her face.

Instantaneously, they both started laughing. A chuckle at first and then a full-blown laugh that came from deep inside her.

Thank you, Lyndon. You've had the last word after all.

PERSPIRATION TRICKLED down Francene's back as she speared the digging fork into the dirt with a grunt.

Despite taking regular breaks and staying inside during the hottest part of the day to continue unpacking boxes and organise her house, her enthusiasm rose with every turn of a sod and her mind raced with planting ideas.

When she returned to the weed-filled bed after four in the afternoon, she stared at the pile of grass and dead plants with satisfaction. Her muscles ached, but with every metre she dug, she revealed another little surprise—a hidden bulb here and there and several rose plants so choked by weeds that it had only been their thorns that gave them away.

It was almost dark as she transferred the weeds into a wheelbarrow she'd found in the garden shed along with a range of tools, when she recognised the sound of a vehicle approaching. *Bryn!*

He pulled into her driveway and slid out of the ute with a wide smile. 'Hope you don't mind a visit at this hour of the day?'

'Of course not. Come in.' She stripped off the gardening gloves and dropped them onto the bottom step. 'I'm ready for a cold drink anyway.'

He followed her through the front room and into the kitchen where she pulled a jug of cold water from the fridge.

'Want one?'

'Sure.'

While she poured, she slid her gaze sideways, noting his damp beard and catching a whiff of shampoo and aftershave.

'How did your family Christmas go?' She indicated the smaller back veranda, now shaded as the sun slipped over the hills in the distance. 'Shall we sit out here? It's lovely at this time of day.'

They sat side-by-side on the top step, and he took a gulp of water before answering. 'Actually, it was better than I'd expected.'

She felt the difference in him from only two days earlier. His tight, anxious face had softened and even his limbs appeared looser. Although he had only walked from the ute to her back porch, his limp was no worse than her own after sitting in one position for too long.

'Tell me more? Did your parents like the seat?'

'Loved it.' He grew solemn for a moment. 'I got a bit of a shock with Dad. He's got Parkinson's. Apparently, he hasn't been too good for a while but was only diagnosed a week ago.'

She rested a hand on his arm. 'Oh, I'm so sorry.' Biting her lip, she remembered the bitterness in his references to his father before Christmas. Did this illness mean his personality had changed as well as his body?

'Yeah. He seems to be taking it better than anyone

thought he would—and his attitude toward me was certainly different.' He snorted. 'Even shook my hand and thanked me for coming. And he was stoked with the seat. Sat in it for ages.'

Flooded with warm relief for him, she squeezed his hand. 'I'm really pleased to hear it.'

While they talked, Francene got up, slid a frozen pizza into the oven, and opened a bottle of wine.

She passed him a glass and once again sat next to him, jumping when her leg brushed against his. Her mind flicked between the burning elation that flashed through her and reminding herself she didn't have a good track record where men were concerned. *Are you sure you want to go there?*

'I really like you, Francene.' Bryn's comment seemed to come from nowhere and yet his reassuringly gentle smile wiped the doubt from her mind.

'I confess—I really like you too.'

They laughed softly, and she regaled the busy, enjoyable Christmas Day she had spent at the farm.

'So, you're not going to hightail it back to the city then?'

Her grin widened. 'No way. This is my home now and I intend to make it everything I've dreamed of.'

His hand rested over the top of hers as he leaned closer. 'Me too.'

39

———————

Two days later, Andrew, Sarah, Ginny, and Kirk sat around the Featherwood Station dining table with a sheaf of papers spread out in front of them.

'So you're happy then?' Andrew asked, his eyes meeting Ginny's. 'Sure you don't want to be the proud owner of a long-lost section of Featherwood Station again?'

'No. I'm delighted that you and your mum can afford it—and you want it. It's a win for us all, really. The original property returns to the family as it was generations ago, and we get to have you as our neighbour permanently.'

'Plus, we also get to have our overseas holiday, which wouldn't be happening if we poured the last of our savings into buying Glenrowan—and had an enormous debt to repay,' Kirk added.

'I think this calls for a bottle of bubbly.' Ginny rose feeling lighter, younger, and blissfully calm. She hadn't experienced a hot flush or a flare of bad temper since Andrew revealed his hopes and they'd discussed options at length.

Now the decision was made. Nigel had accepted Andrew's and Sarah's generous offer, and the paperwork had been signed. Although not intending to have anything to do with the physical labour or employment of workers, Sarah had pointed out that Andrew was her only child and would eventually inherit her estate. Her contribution would be as a business partner and advisor, and as an accountant, she would take care of the bookkeeping for as long as she could.

'I have advised Nigel I'll be dropping these documents off with our solicitor as soon as they reopen after the new year,' Sarah said. 'He had confirmed he and his friend will leave for Tasmania tomorrow and he will deal with his side of things via email.'

Ginny placed a stemmed glass in front of each of them while Kirk opened the bottle of bubbles.

Then, with glasses filled and raised, they each gave a toast.

'To new beginnings,' Andrew said.

'To the reunion and future of Featherwood Station,' Ginny added.

Sarah grinned. 'To us all.'

And Kirk stood and faced the photo of Lyndon and his prize-winning bull that had hung on the wall for years. 'Thanks, mate. I never met you, but if it wasn't for your unfortunate circumstances, this home would not be filled with our love and happiness. This one's for you.'

Ginny blinked surprised tears away and took a gulp of her wine. Kirk was right. It was a happy home and both she and her daughters were fortunate to have found love. While her mind drifted, Andrew plonked his empty glass on the table and pushed his chair back.

'Are you all coming to the hangi at the pub on New Year's Eve?'

'Count me out,' Sarah said. 'I'm going to a Chamber of Commerce dinner party.'

Kirk chuckled. 'Probably a bit more upmarket than what we'll be enjoying, but Sam wanted to do something in true kiwi style before he and Sophie head over the ditch to meet his parents.'

'I thought you were invited to Ashleigh and Damian's wedding?' Ginny said, looking at Andrew.

'Yeah. I have been. It won't be a big affair though, and it's in the late morning too, with lunch afterwards. Mainly Ashleigh's family and a few friends, I think. Damian said around twenty-five all up. Apparently, Francene's making the cake, which will be dessert, and as you know, Alex and Briony are in charge of the entrée and main courses.'

'Sounds lovely,' Ginny said quietly, having gathered her scattered emotions once again. 'Knowing Valerie and Neil, it will be beautiful with flowers everywhere and not a thing forgotten.' She reflected on the couple who had purchased the home and garden years earlier before turning it into a stunning wedding venue and becoming firm friends of hers and Kirk's.

'Probably,' Andrew said. 'And as Ashleigh's family is heading back to Brisbane afterwards for some big New Year's bash they always attend, I reckon most other guests will join us at the pub.'

Kirk looked at his watch. 'If you're right, I guess I'd better get myself down there to give the fellas a hand to dig the hangi. From what he said the other day, he's got it all planned and is pretty excited about putting it on for everyone.'

'I don't think I've ever tried food cooked that way,' Ginny said. 'Did you say they put a fire into the ground?'

'Sort of. The traditional Māori way is to dig a pit in the ground and build a large fire nearby to heat a pile of volcanic rocks. When it's hot, they lay the stones in the bottom of the pit and place the baskets of food lined with leaves or aluminium foil on top. Then they cover the entire setup with earth, trapping the heat and steam inside for hours. When it's ready to open, you lift the baskets out and the meat or fish just falls off the bone. The vegetables have a beautiful, earthy flavour.' He pursed his lips and gave a chef's kiss.

'Can't wait.' Ginny raised her eyebrows and grinned. 'It sounds like a good way to say goodbye to this year and welcome in the next.'

SMOKE WAFTED through the air as the crowd grew, their glasses clinking and voices rising in conversation on the back deck of Featherwood Falls Hotel.

Sweat poured off Sam as he supervised Kirk, Bruce, and Rhys in lifting the feast from the hot tomb below.

'This sure is a change from Hogmanay,' Bruce said to no one in particular. His face reddened with the heat and his smile grew.

Aileen hovered near the pit, clearly fascinated by the whole event, while Briony, Ginny, and Sophie organised covers for the outdoor trestle tables and fetched large roasting pans and serving platters from the kitchen. Plates, cutlery, and napkins were added to the essentials and half an hour later, the meal was ready.

The crowd was not as big as Ginny had expected but, she reasoned, many families had gone on their summer holidays and were probably sitting by the sea somewhere, hoping the weather stayed fine while they saw the new year in.

Clapping sounded from inside the hotel and moments before the first person in the queue helped themselves, Damian and Ashleigh appeared, hand in hand, wearing their wedding attire and with young Charlie proudly leading them into the milling crowd.

'Woo-hoo!' someone yelled.

'Congratulations,' another voice added.

Eleanor stood nearest to them, her friend Tim, the man from Tenterfield who had befriended her and helped her find her ancestry, beside her. Francene and Bryn pressed against the wall of the hotel while Emma rocked Liam in the pram and Ryan, Frank, and Sam ran a temporary fence around the empty pit to protect anyone from getting too close as it cooled down.

The hours flew, the voices and music growing louder until, minutes before midnight, Alex added more wood to the fire and everyone gathered around it, waiting for the final countdown.

When it began, the residents of Featherwood Falls, friends, Scottish relatives, and anyone else who happened to be in the area for the evening, joined in, shouting the descending numbers and then, at the crack of Kirk's stockwhip, a cheer went up, startling any sleeping dogs in the town.

Bryn wrapped Francene in a hug and kissed her— first gently on the cheek and then, as their lips met, clearly oblivious to those around them, their kiss deepened.

On the other side of the roaring fire, Kirk slid his arm around Ginny's waist, drawing her away and raising his face to the sky. 'We've both had some bumps in the road over these last few years, but I reckon our time has come. Let's make this year ours—to love, live, and enjoy every day that we have.'

She leaned her head on his shoulder, her heart full. 'I couldn't have said it better.'

EPILOGUE

Six months had passed since new year, and Ginny sang as she gathered clothes from the drawers, lay them out, then rolled them neatly and placed them in the individual packing pouches. Satisfied she had thought of every eventuality, she scanned her list and ticked items off, chuckling at the realisation that Briony's "list" habit had somehow been adopted by them all. Parkas, wet-weather pants and raincoats (just in case it was colder or wetter than they expected), warm layers and cool, summery T-shirts, slacks and dresses for her and shorts for Kirk.

Reassured Canada and Alaska looked good in July, she couldn't wait. Despite Kirk moaning he could buy a brand-new vehicle for the cost of their holiday, he had worn a smile for days now as each hour grew closer. A wave of anxiety washed over her occasionally, quickly dissipated by excitement.

'Don't worry about a thing,' Claire said, patting her growing tummy. 'Baby and I will take care of every-thing here and it's come at a perfect time for us. By the time you get home, Bryn will have moved out and we'll have our house to ourselves.'

'And Rhys is happy with the new constable?'

'Yes. He said he's switched on and keen but has a bit to learn about country policing. At least he's getting well fed at the pub, unlike poor Rhys was.' She giggled. 'Remember how he hated Ned's stews—especially three or more times a week. I don't think he's eaten one since.'

'I'm pleased for you, love. Everything's working out well—and something tells me I'll have more than one grandchild arriving in this next year.'

Claire grinned. 'Yep. Briony's getting all clucky now. When she went to Warwick to collect supplies last week, she came home with more baby clothes for us. This child will be the best-dressed kid in Featherwood Falls.'

'Oh well. I guess she has time to think about it now. I'm so pleased they've employed more staff. Julia seems very pleasant—and efficient. And taking on school-leavers for work experience is not only helpful to Briony and Alex but also good for the kids. Even if they find other work or study something else, hopefully they'll have some idea about cooking and running a business.'

Claire voiced her agreement, adding, 'Too true. I'll head off now, Mum, but I'll be back tomorrow to run through any last-minute concerns you have.'

She kissed her mother on the cheek and strode out of the bedroom.

As her footsteps faded, a soft smile spread over Ginny's face and anticipation warmed her insides.

The year had started with good rain, fluctuating crop and stock prices seemed to have stabilised, at least for the moment, and the winter had been kind.

Now all she and Kirk had to do was enjoy this trip of a lifetime and make wonderful memories, knowing that whatever they'd left behind would be cared for.

I can do that.

BRYN WANDERED around the enormous shed with pride, the blue heeler dog at his heels and his arm loose around Francene's waist.

At one end, a small bathroom, kitchen, and one-room living-come-sleeping area were partitioned off in the building's interior, with sliding glass doors leading from the living quarters to the outside. On the interior wall, a solid timber door opened into the shed where a large kennel sat on its own platform, filled with a squishy bed and with the name "Digger" emblazoned above the doggy door.

Across on the opposite side of the building, another room with a wooden floor held Bryn's lathe, benches, and equipment needed for his business.

Orders had flowed after the word had spread and people had seen his various pieces of furniture outside the general store, Francene's cottage, and the hotel. Now he had enough incoming work to keep him busy for months. New ideas also presented themselves when he least expected them, buoying him on as much as Francene's admiration did.

He led her outside with Digger following, and they stared down the valley where afternoon sunlight slanted through tall trees. A soft winter fog formed over the river, and he let his shoulders sag.

This was what he'd dreamed of. A small property of his own where he could run a few animals to keep it tidy and provide a little extra income, and a decent shed in which to create his never-ending dreams.

Although the shed was not big enough for him and Francene to live in permanently, further plans to build a house on the adjacent patch of level ground filled him with hope and excitement. For the moment though, he was comfortable with their arrangements. He would stay with her in her cottage a couple of nights through the week, she would come to the small-holding when she wasn't too busy, and in time, their lives would meld into whatever life was destined to be. One he hoped saw them living together in their new home.

'I love it,' she whispered. 'And I know your parents will too.'

His heart swelled with pride. Although his father's health was deteriorating, he had phoned Bryn for a chat every week or two—not one where he criticised or domineered but one filled with genuine interest about Bryn's progress and next project. They had already visited Featherwood Falls twice, voiced their approval of Francene—not that he required it, but regardless, he had been pleased to receive it—and had promised to return soon. A year ago, he would never have dreamed his life could have experienced such change. But now, anything was possible and his future held hope, love, and happiness.

DAYS LATER, Francene closed the doors against the chill of the approaching evening and retreated to the kitchen.

She would prepare the pastry dough for tomorrow and make gnocchi for hers and Eleanor's dinner, then she would ring Bryn to see how his day had been.

Her first six months operating "Tea, Tarts and Treasures" had begun slowly, but within a month, she had discovered she needed another pair of hands as its clientele rapidly increased. A random enquiry from a new resident in town, Eloise, had provided the opportunity Francene needed. Although a casual employee, Eloise had quickly proved she was enthusiastic, reliable, and cheerful. Her skills included marketing and sales, and within a couple of weeks, she had opened a social media page for Francene and convinced her she needed a website. With limited experience in the field, Francene had happily followed her employee's advice, had commissioned a local techno-whizz to create the website, and learned how to post daily on her social media account. That, plus the spreading local enthusiasm, had drawn a steadily growing custom—one that kept Francene busier than she had ever imagined.

With the opening of Francene's facilities, Lola had reduced the quantity of homemade lamingtons and pies and welcomed Janet and Ryan's ideas of producing fresh salads and burgers, providing a contrasting menu from both Francene's business and the hotel. It seemed to work well, with visitors often having lunch at the store's small café corner, afternoon tea at "Tea, Tarts and Treasures", and then having dinner and a night's accommodation at the hotel. Francene wondered how they ate so much—but she didn't mind. It was great for the town and fabulous for all the local businesses.

A knock on the door startled her as she wrapped the last of the pastry and placed it in the fridge.

After hurrying to the front door, she opened it before drawing Eleanor inside and quickly closing it again.

'Ooh, it's so cosy in here,' Eleanor said.

'Isn't it?' Francene moved to the fire and added another piece of wood—courtesy of Bryn.

With the new drapes Francene had purchased to fit with the historic cottage vibe closed, the warmth enveloped them.

'I'm sorry now that I didn't have a combustion heater installed,' Eleanor said. 'With the solar panels on the roof, I thought electricity would be easier and less work. And it is. Only ... nothing feels quite as homely as a good wood fire.'

'But you're happy in your new home?'

'Oh yes. I love it. And it's so nice to not be travelling back and forth to Brisbane. But you know how it is—there's always something we have to compromise on.'

Francene nodded enthusiastically. In her case, it was deciding how best to run both hers and Bryn's businesses satisfactorily without leaving either property vulnerable to unwanted visitors—or worse.

'One day soon, I'll live with Bryn in our own house on his little farm and employ someone to work with me and live in my cottage in a sort of caretaker role.'

'I think that sounds very wise.' Eleanor smiled at

her. 'It's quite extraordinary really—less than a year ago we were both living in Brisbane, neither of us particularly happy and with more worries than we could cope with. Now here we are in this pretty little town—you with a gorgeous cottage and running a business you have dreamed of for years. Not to mention finding love,' she added. 'And me in my bright, new house with lovely neighbours and everything I need within walking distance.'

Nodding, Francene's gaze met hers and they chuckled. 'And all because of you falling on those concrete steps.'

Eleanor smiled again, and Francene reached out and squeezed her hand. 'I've made gnocchi with mushroom and tomato sauce for dinner—and we have one of my vanilla slices each for dessert.'

The elderly lady raised her eyebrows. 'Absolutely perfect.'

Kirk loaded the second suitcase into the car and waited while Ginny gave Claire, Briony, and the cats each a last hug.

'Bye, darlings. See you in six weeks.'

'See you, Mum. Don't worry about anything here,' Claire said.

'Yes. And send us photos and a few quick words

whenever you can—but don't spend hours doing it. Your holiday is to be enjoyed, not spent sending messages,' Briony added firmly.

'I get it. Nothing to worry about, messages and photos when doing nothing else—and seeing and doing everything we can fit in.'

'You've got it,' Claire said as Ginny got into the car.

Ginny waved through the open window as they pulled away, her stomach whirling and filled with a mix of excitement, anxiety, and apprehension.

Had she forgotten anything?

She looked at her watch, estimating they would reach Brisbane midafternoon, allowing time to book into their airport hotel and stroll to a nearby centre for dinner. Their flight didn't leave until eleven the following morning, but she knew better than to be too complacent. When living hours from the airport, anything could happen, and she refused to allow this trip to be spoiled.

Kirk reached his hand out to hers, and she clutched it.

'This is it,' he said. 'You, me, and the opportunity of a lifetime. This time tomorrow, we'll be up there and on our way to Canada. It will be perfect.'

As she looked into his deep blue eyes, soft with love and trust, she breathed deeply and returned his smile.

'Yes, it will.'

THE END

AFTERWORD

If you enjoyed this book, I would love you to leave a review on your preferred site. Reviews encourage authors to continue writing and also help other readers to find my books. Thank you for reading "A Festive Featherwood Falls".

ALSO BY HEATHER REYBURN

Tullagulla Series

The Cedar Tree

The English Oak

The Pepperina Grove

A Tullagulla Christmas

Fantail Ridge Series

Peninsula Promises

The Lupin Fields

The Scent of Promise

Featherwood Falls Series

A Stranger in Featherwood Falls

Secrets in Featherwood Falls

Sparks Fly in Featherwood Falls

Clouds over Featherwood Falls

Coming Home to Featherwood Falls

A Festive Featherwood Falls

ACKNOWLEDGMENTS

To my super-supportive husband and sisters, my early (BETA) readers and my ARC readers - I value your encouragement, support and honest critique above all else and thank you from the bottom of my heart. Your suggestions, constructive comments and tolerance make the relatively lonely career of writing worthwhile.

A special thank you to my friend Des who was kind enough to share his on-farm accident with me, an experience he was happy for me to use in this story.

To Anna and Lauren at CREATINGink, thank you both for editing my books. Your professional assistance and ongoing friendship is very much appreciated.

Patti Roberts at Paradox Book Cover Designs—thank you again for your gorgeous covers and so much more.

Readers, I hope you have enjoyed reuniting with the Featherwood Falls community and enjoy this festive season with them, despite a few "bumps in the road".

Thank you for your ongoing support and encouragement - and for reading my books.

A STRANGER IN FEATHERWOOD FALLS

To lose a loved one is tragic, but to lose a lifetime of dreams? Unthinkable.

Alone on a two thousand hectare sheep and cattle property, Ginny Shepherd questions her husband's sudden death, convinced it was no accident. As a series of farm related incidents unravel, heightening her suspicions, her livelihood is put under threat. Featherwood Station is Ginny's lifeblood—her passion, her home, and her haven and she is determined it will stay that way. But it seems someone else wants the property as much as she does and will stop at nothing to get it.

When a stranger finds a forgotten token gifted to him as a child, distant memories set him on a path to pursue his grandfather's dream. But, greeted with more questions than answers, he finds life in the heart of

Queensland's Granite Belt more difficult than expected.

A smouldering attraction forms between he and Ginny, alarm bells sound and frightening events escalate. Ginny's life is in danger.

Is the stranger who he says he is? Or could it be that someone has a grudge to settle?

SECRETS IN FEATHERWOOD FALLS

A small country town. A conscientious cop. And a whole lot of secrets.

Constable Rhys Morton is new to Featherwood Falls and knows one thing for certain—he wants to remain in this village as much as he wants to remain a cop. But just as he uncovers troubling historical information, an accusation threatens his security and he must weigh up his options. Should he pursue the cold case and risk ruffling powerful feathers, or protect his future and a budding romance?

Claire Shepherd is still reeling from her father's death and when fresh heartbreak strikes, she seeks peace in the haven of Featherwood Station, her childhood home. Sparks fly between Claire and the new cop in town and she is torn between her dream of managing her father's legacy or falling for a man whose position is only temporary.

Alarm bells chime when new neighbours move in. Is this little town the sleepy hollow Rhys believed it to be? Desperate to uncover local secrets, he seeks Claire's help. After all, she knows the area and he has nothing to lose—except his heart.

Secrets is Rhys and Claire's story and the second in the Featherwood Falls series.

SPARKS FLY OVER FEATHERWOOD FALLS

Fed up with life under scrutiny, Ashleigh Paton considers her grandmother's favourite saying—*"Escape to the Country! A Change is as good as a holiday."*

The advice ignites a yearning in Ashleigh to leave city life and all it involves. A teaching position in Featherwood Falls could provide the answer, one she hopes will offer the new life she craves. After all—what could go wrong? It's better than being unemployed and the reward could be the peace she desires.

Damian Cartwright has a secret. Like his eccentric great-aunt, a reclusive life in the bush suits him. Except now his son, Charlie, is old enough to start school, and old enough to be subjected to ridicule. It's time for action, even if that involves calling a truce with Charlie's feisty new teacher.

When unexplained events occur in the area, young

Charlie forces Ashleigh into seeking answers. But uncovering the truth proves more shocking than imagined and sparks fly in more ways than one.

Can Ashleigh extinguish the inferno without destroying all she has gained? Or will her dreams be over before they begin?

Sparks Fly in Featherwood Falls is the third book in this series.

CLOUDS OVER FEATHERWOOD FALLS

In a town teaming with secrets, three women find themselves inexplicably entwined.

At the edge of her future, sixteen-year-old **Zoe** teeters, uncertain. The vibrant city with its dazzling lights, familiar sounds and scents, and close friends exudes adventure and a dream career. But when unexpected tragedy strikes, she is left to navigate the world on her own, gripped by loneliness and fear.

Lola is feeling the weight of her years. Despite a loving husband, a flourishing business and a circle of faithful friends, she's missing something. While she pours her soul into a menagerie of sick and abandoned animals, her heart aches for the return of her only child.

At forty-two and feeling lonely, **Emma** is free at last. Lost love and an unwavering commitment to her late mother have confined her to the quiet charm of Featherwood Falls. And while her role as teacher's aide at the local school fills her days, she longs for something to happen—something that will transform her existence and redefine her life.

Can Featherwood Falls offer the key to uniting these women? Or will a dangerous voice from the past destroy family bonds, challenging the discovery of love and hope.

COMING HOME TO FEATHERWOOD FALLS

Adrift after a series of disappointments, Briony Shepherd finds herself at a crossroad. To remain in a job that has lost its shine or to make a new life elsewhere.

Her hometown beckons, and amidst the vast landscapes of country Queensland, Featherwood Falls becomes the haven she needed.

As she and her fiancé embrace a life-changing opportunity, the arrival of carefree travellers infuses new energy into the town, igniting hope, a sense of kinship ... and intrigue.

But when a visitor arrives, hidden secrets surface and Briony's newfound venture is challenged by an unimaginable historical tragedy.

Featherwood Falls, with its enigmatic charm, becomes

the setting for an enthralling tale of love, resilience, and the courage to embrace unforeseen beginnings.

ABOUT THE AUTHOR

Heather Reyburn enjoyed an idyllic childhood in beautiful New Zealand, before settling on the Darling Downs in Queensland. With a passion for nature, animals, reading and all things farm related, it wasn't long before her rural lifestyle inspired dreams of writing stories of her own. She loves happy endings, history, suspense, and characters who remain with the reader long after "The End". When not writing, Heather is often found in the garden or spending time with her husband and family.

www.ingramcontent.com/pod-product-compliance
Lightning Source LLC
Chambersburg PA
CBHW030525120726
47904CB00005B/1623